A Brush With Love,
A Brush With The Law

Summer Augustine

PEARL ROSE
PUBLISHING

ACKNOWLEDGEMENTS

This book is dedicated to my wonderful friends, and my sister, who encouraged me throughout the process. Thank you, Cynthia, Cecilia, and Kimberly.

TABLE OF CONTENTS

CHAPTER 1

"David crashed another Lamborghini tonight."

"What! What the fuck! Was he drinking and driving again?!"

"No, he said there was water on the road... "

"How could there be water on the road?! It's July! We haven't had rain in months!"

"Dear, he was..."

"No! Stop!"

"He said somebody's pool..."

"No. Stop defending him. You always defend him. That's why he's like this, you know. If he was just half as bright as those damn yellow Lamborghinis he always drives! And why are they always yellow! Aren't sports cars supposed to be red! --"

"Dear, please calm down."

"How can I calm down? All you've ever done is defend his misbehavior. He could've killed someone. He could've killed himself. How would you feel then, huh? Would it make you feel better to tell a stupid story about a pool, and water on the road at his funeral? Would denying that he killed himself drinking and driving, make you feel better at his funeral?!"

"Darling, nobody's dead. Please calm down. It's just a wrecked car."

"You know his siblings, *our children*, look up to him. They see his reckless behavior and they follow it. Because he is so 'cool.' "

"*Our children?* Why emphasize the word '*our?*' Is David a castaway compared to them!?"

"No, you know I didn't mean that."

"You've always treated him different. When I was a single mother, you promised me that when we got married and had children together, you wouldn't treat him different. I trusted you. All his life, I've had to defend him from your unfair treatment."

"Different!? How can you say that? I pulled every string to get him into that Ivy League school. I spent hundreds of thousands of dollars in donations, as if he were my own son. But he refused to go! He just pissed that away for his partying lifestyle!"

"Money. It always comes down to money and status for you. You just don't ever think about love."

David Nolan could hear his mother and stepfather arguing down the hall. He wished there was other noise in the house so he didn't have to hear it go on. He always came to his mother's house when he was sick or injured. There was nothing like his mother's care to make him strong again. This time, the injuries really laid him up. No broken bones, just scrapes and bruises all over his body. But it hurt to move an inch. So he just lay on his back and didn't bother getting up to grab the remote to turn on the TV. He wished his mother had remembered to bring it to the nightstand next to the bed when she'd come in to take away his dinner tray. He wanted to drown out their argument more than anything, but it hurt even more to move. So, he just lay there.

David had heard many arguments over him between his mother and stepfather, growing up. And it didn't hurt any less now that he was a grown man, nearly 30 years old. Hearing his stepfather's anger always made him miss his biological father so much. Why had God given him such little time to spend with his father? He was just a boy, only six years old when his father passed away. But he remembered him, remembered his booming voice. It was always booming with joy. He was a jolly man, a loving man. He lit up the room with warmth and laughter. Everyone loved his father. Especially him.

David's father was an icon to him, a God almost. He was ripped away from him in a terrible car accident when David was just six years old. He'll never forget that day. It was New Year's Eve. And for the first time, his parents were going to allow him to stay up until midnight with them. His mother was home preparing the decorations. It was getting late but his mother told him to be patient because father had some serious business to take care of before coming home to celebrate. But it was already 10:00 p.m. and David was anxious, "When's daddy coming home?" He would ask every 10 minutes. His mom tried to distract him with the television, but every time a commercial came on, he would ask again: "When's daddy coming home?" His mother knew it could be late, but didn't think he would be later than 10:30. She knew her husband was excited to spend his son's first New Year's Eve that he would stay up for. He said it was the first New Year's Eve his son would be old enough to remember. He wanted to make it special and celebrate at home, just the family. They were going to watch the ball drop on TV.

He and his wife would have Champagne, the boy would have sparkling cider, and the three of them were going to toast at midnight. It wasn't like him to be this late, especially a night he had been so looking forward to. Around 11:00 p.m., David's mother began to seriously worry. She tried not to show her worry, but David could tell his mother seemed unhappy about something. Maybe she wanted daddy to come home, too. As each minute passed by, David became more and more disappointed. "Why isn't daddy here, mommy?" he asked, sadly. "He's going to miss the toast." Little David pouted. They both watched the clock. It was 5 minutes to midnight now, and not a word from his father. Then, as the ball started dropping, and the people on TV were counting backwards, there was a knock at the door. It was two police officers. David did not know why, upon first sight of the police officers, his mother dropped to the floor, crying and sobbing uncontrollably. They seemed nice and they hadn't made a move toward her. Then, one of them spoke: "We are sorry to inform you ma'am. There has been an accident..." Little David didn't understand all the words the police officer said that night, but he did understand one word: "died."

David often wondered what his father would think of him now. Would he fault him for "pissing away" an Ivy League education, as his stepfather put it? Or would he be proud of him for making his own way, not accepting any handouts from another man who was not his father? David refused to go to the college his stepfather chose for him because he couldn't accept anything from a man who treated him like he was second-class to his other siblings. But he probably shouldn't have lied about it. After high school, David pretended that he enrolled because he didn't want to go through another battle. He gave a great speech at the family dinner celebration after graduation, expressing the utmost gratitude for his stepfather's efforts that got him in to an Ivy League school, which was sure to guaranty his success in life. His mother smiled up at him proudly as he gave that toast, and everyone raised their glasses.

But instead of heading off to college, David headed off to New York, hell-bent on making it on his own. He knew about the stock exchange, and he had heard about the fast money a young, ambitious man could make. It was perfect timing. On his 18th birthday, the small inheritance from his father's death became available to him. It was enough to fund a tiny apartment in Manhattan for 3 months with a little left over to invest.

David knew he only had 3 months to either make it or break it. David was lucky. He made a lot of money fast. He kept reinvesting his earnings, like playing the house's money in Vegas. By his 19th birthday, David was a millionaire. He stayed in New York long enough to make many millions of dollars. Then he moved back to L.A. where he began investing in the movie business and made many millions more.

David now had a mansion in Malibu, a modest 4,000 square foot house in Beverly Hills, and a grand party house in the Hollywood Hills. Many would find that lifestyle ridiculously excessive -- having 3 large homes within a 20-mile radius. Certainly, his stepfather had expressed his disgust with such excess. His stepfather thought a man should be more responsible, more honorable, leading a conservative, respectable lifestyle that didn't involve nightly parties and excessive waste. However, David thought it was all necessary. An outsider viewing what appeared to be a hard-partying lifestyle didn't understand that this was Hollywood's method of "networking." Just as doctors and lawyers gather at boring conferences, Hollywood calls for excessive, wild parties that gather the biggest names in the movie industry where movie deals are made during conversations surrounded by loud music, loose women, booze, and even cocaine (though David did not partake in the last indulgence mentioned). David collected many sports cars because a showing of wealth was necessary to maintain an image that gained the level of respect necessary to conduct business in Hollywood. Just as a lawyer must maintain a closet full of suits necessary to impress judges, juries and clients, David needed a collection of sports cars.

Of course, he loved his toys for the pure thrill and enjoyment they offered too. His favorite sports car was a lightening yellow Lamborghini. He usually drove yellow Lamborghinis. He loved the color. It reminded him of the brightness of the sun. It also suited his personality very well. David was a vivacious, life-of-the-party kind of guy. He was always smiling and happy. He could gather a crowd with his warm, welcoming personality. He could be loud, but it was never obnoxious. He drew the attention of all around him, and his audience loved him. Complete strangers would warm up to him easily. He could make a group of strangers feel like they were long lost friends enjoying each other's company, as they gathered around the nucleus of David's personality. This personality also helped David get lucky with the ladies -- every time. Certainly his wealth played a role, but he didn't need that. He was a natural charmer.

Each of David's homes served a very different purpose. The Malibu mansion was his sanctuary. It was the place he would retreat to in order to find peace and solace from his hectic lifestyle. The panoramic ocean view that encircled the entire front of his mansion put him at ease. The sound of the ocean and the view of waves rolling towards him would always wash away any stress or troubled feelings that life would sometimes bring. This is the place he would come, to gather strength, think, and just relax. This was truly his home. It was where his heart was. Only his closest friends and relatives were invited to his Malibu mansion. He never brought a romantic partner there, in case things ended badly. He wanted his sanctuary protected from angry, jilted lovers. So, he simply hid it from all his lovers. The only woman he would ever bring to his sanctuary, would be the one he would make his wife. Though David loved his partying lifestyle, and he loved the women that came with it, deep down David wanted one special woman to share his life with. Though he never admitted this to anyone, he believed that his wealth was meant to be shared with his wife and the future family they would make together. He wanted someone to share it all with. He wanted someone who could enjoy it with him. He wanted a marriage that would last forever. He wanted all of his children to be full-siblings with no step-parents. This made it very difficult to find the right woman. How could he ever know that a relationship would last a lifetime? How would he ever find the woman who makes him want to be with her forever? David had no strategy for achieving his heart's desire. Instead, he just continued on the treadmill of changing lovers and indulging in the fast-life that brought fast-women. It was a hard habit to break.

David's house in the Hollywood Hills, was just that; a house in the Hollywood Hills. It was the place he threw outrageous parties with hundreds of guests. The parties would last all night long. He would spend most of his nights there because his lifestyle truly was a never-ending party. The many women he entertained (and who entertained him) in his bedroom would spend their nights with him in the Hollywood Hills. Usually, it was a different woman (or set of women), each night.

David's modest home in the flats of Beverly Hills, was necessary for convenience. Most of his business dinners and meetings with lawyers took place in Beverly Hills. These meetings would last well into the night and often times involved heavy consumption of alcohol. It was most convenient to click a single button on his cell phone to order an Uber Ride to drive him just a few blocks to a home where he would get a good night's sleep, after a long meeting. The Beverly Hills home also served as his business headquarters. It was where he kept his home-office (which would not be appropriately placed in his party house and would only serve to ruin his sanctuary). It was also conveniently located and easily accessible to his personal assistant, who he usually needed handy and available around the clock. One bedroom was specifically reserved for her in case she had to stay overnight. David had one very strict rule. He never became romantically involved with any of his staff. It was not the potential for a sexual harassment lawsuit that concerned him, as he had plenty of money to deal with lawsuits. He simply thought it was stupid to lose good staff over a short-lived romantic fling. They were far more valuable to him as trusted employees.

After David overheard the argument between his mother and his stepfather, David decided he would rather recover at his home in Beverly

Hills, where his staff could tend to his needs. It would hurt his mother's feelings that he would not stay and allow her to take care of him; so, he would make an excuse and pretend he had important documents to review before an important teleconference he had the next day. He knew his mother would make daily visits and that was good enough to make them both feel better. So he called his assistant Katrina and asked her to come pick him up.

After about three weeks of rest and recovery, David began to get bored. He was back to 100% now and he wanted to go out on the town. So, he called his old friend, Frank: "Hey, meet me at Lola's in Hollywood."

CHAPTER 2

Sarah Cartwright was a virgin; the apple of her parents' eye. She grew up in a small conservative town, surrounded by people with strong family values. Without a doubt, in her mind, she would stay a virgin until she was married. The hard part was finding a man who thought that was a good idea. With a population of less than 2,000 people, the town she grew up in had 10 churches. She grew up working the morning shift of her parent's restaurant, serving breakfast to churchgoers every Sunday. As a child, she had dreamed of becoming an attorney, like she'd seen in Perry Mason re-runs. Her idol had been "Paige" from that show "Dynasty" or was it Falcon Crest? She couldn't remember now – it was one of those late night soap operas her mother watched every week. She wasn't even certain she was remembering the character "Paige" correctly.

Although she was influenced by television characters she grew up watching as a child, she wasn't sure her current grown-up memory of the character was accurate. It wasn't until she was in an interview at a District Attorney's Office during law school, that she realized Perry Mason was a defense attorney, not a prosecutor in that show. All she remembered was how he'd always get a confession out of someone during cross-examination. And that's the kind of prosecutor she always wanted to be when she grew up -- the kind she prided herself in being today.

All Sarah remembered about the character "Paige" was that she was a gorgeous woman in a power suit who always seemed to have the upper hand in every conversation. Growing up in the '80s, there weren't very many female characters on TV who were depicted as young, beautiful, strong and successful like Paige. Back then it was the blonde damsel in distress who got the hero in the end. But Sarah didn't want to be a damsel in distress saved by a hero. She wanted to have her own power, her own independence and her own success. Growing up, her friends would say: " I'm going to marry a rich guy one day." She would say, "Not me! I'm the one who is going to be rich." And now, after all her hard work studying, getting a scholarship at an Ivy League college and graduating law school, Sarah sat at her desk around midnight in the District Attorney's Office, earning the measly salary of a public servant. It was another long day of fighting crime.

She knew that working in the District Attorney's Office would never make her rich. But oh,... the glory. The glory of winning one trial after another, fighting the good fight was what Sarah worked for now. The personal satisfaction of getting the bad guys off the street, had its own rewards, which could never be matched with money or the luxuries money could buy. No, she wouldn't consider taking a job at that white collar crime defense firm that kept courting her, offering her higher and higher pay, enticing her with luxury automobiles as a signing bonus. Though, she did ask herself one day: "If they knew my weakness for bright yellow Lamborghinis, and offered me that car, would I cave in?" She pushed the thought away and promised herself to keep that a secret so they wouldn't add that to their list of offerings. She didn't want to be tempted. She didn't want to "sell out." She didn't believe she could ever compromise her high moral standards and unyielding integrity by representing a criminal, no matter how "white" his crime was.

No, she would never let White, White & Smith tempt her out of her dedication to fighting the good fight. She always had to laugh at the thought of that law firm's name. Why didn't they just pretend like old Smith's last name was "Collar" They could've named their firm, "White, Collar" so all those millionaire thieves wouldn't have to think too hard to remember who to call when they got caught. Just then, the phone rang. *How coincidental, it was White, Sr. Was it telepathy? Did her thoughts of his firm, make him call her?* She knew that was a silly thought, but just in case, she tried to force herself not to think about yellow Lamborghinis.

"How's the toughest, DA, in the country?" he asked.

"How did you know I'd be here?" she said.

"Where else would you be!? Ha, ha, ha. You and me both kid, we're still at the office."

Sarah then replied: "Yeah, but my work will get me another win on my win-loss record. It doesn't matter how late you work, your guilty client will still be guilty."

"Ha, ha, ha. It doesn't matter if he's guilty, only that I can get the jury to like him! I can work with that for an acquittal! Why don't you come work for me? It's not that bad representing the guilty. It's not much different from what you do. After you convict them, they serve their sentences, they get out, they do it again! So what's the point? Come work for me. At least all your hard work will pay off, you'll live a life of luxury."

"Maybe try me when I'm older and wiser."

"Ok. When's your next birthday? I'll have them pick you up in your signing bonus. What color do you like? Red? Red is the best color on a Ferrari."

Sarah smiled and thought to herself, "Don't think of yellow Lamborghinis. Ooops. No, don't think that. Cake! Think of cake, I actually wish I had some chocolate cake, right now."

Then she said: "No signing bonus necessary. Just bring me a chocolate birthday cake. We'll discuss a plea bargain in the Miller case after I blow out the candles."

"You're a tough nut to crack, Madame DA, but I won't give up. Have a good night."

"Good night."

On her way home that night, Sarah thought she'd stop for an apple martini. She drove her old Chrysler Sebring (not fancy, but at least it was a convertible), to Lola's where someone once told her that's where martinis were invented. Could that be true? Was there one place where it all began? That really seemed silly, but she liked repeating that silly little fact to everyone she brought to Lola's. But tonight, she'd be drinking alone.

As Sarah walked into Lola's, David and his cohorts walked out. With two men standing between them, Sarah never saw David. But inexplicably, in that moment that David and Sarah passed by each other, Sarah felt a sudden yearning for someone she missed dearly. It was a deep and desperate feeling, overwhelming her heart. It hit her like a ton of bricks. But she couldn't figure out who she was missing. "*How odd,*" she thought. "*I'm missing someone, but I can't identify who? It must be this damn job,*" she thought to herself. *"I'm working too hard. It's making me go a little crazy. Maybe I'll have 2 martinis tonight. Who knows, maybe my future husband will sit next to me after the bartender pours my second drink."*

Sarah sat at the bar and ordered her drink. As she watched the bartender shake the ingredients of her apple martini, she silently made a promise to herself to find time to develop her social life.

As David and his friends drove further and further away from Lola's Bar, loneliness set in to Sarah's heart. The loneliness Sarah felt grew more and more onerous with each mile David traveled away from Lola's Bar. Sarah sipped her apple martini sadly, at the bar alone, while life went on all around her. She heard a girl next to her giggling at the male attention she was receiving. She heard another man at the end of the bar deliver a pick up line to a tall, skinny blonde. She heard a group of friends behind her, roaring with laughter at a joke one of them made. And she sat alone in silence, staring straight ahead, just sipping her drink. Despite being in a crowded room, the loneliness engulfed her. She then decided one drink was enough. She would close her tab and head home soon.

The next morning Sarah got up to do it all over again. She brushed her teeth, wound her hair up in a tight bun and slipped into one of her power suits. This one was a black, three-piece pantsuit with pinstripes so subtle they were hardly noticeable. It was a sharp suit that commanded respect. It was tapered just right and appeared to have been custom-made, but it was not so tapered that it showed off Sarah's curves. Sarah had naturally large breasts, a small waist and voluptuous hips, with a firm round bottom.

Though she didn't know it, Sarah was a typical bombshell. But Sarah worked hard to cover up those sexy curves. She was a Deputy District Attorney and she wanted to be respected for her mind. She was careful to select suits that hid the size of her breasts in comparison with her small waist. She did this so well, that when she looked in the mirror, she believed she was overweight. She did not look overweight to others, but she grew up during a time before Beyoncé and J.Lo., were part of the media's presentation of the image of beauty. Sarah was left with a misguided perception of her body due to her mother's constant nagging that she diet, combined with the fact that her formative years occurred during a time before the famous song "I like big butts, and I cannot lie" took to airwaves. Sarah always considered herself a little fat. Her body image couldn't be shaken by new concepts of beauty presented in the media during her late high school, early college years. She never considered herself sexy. She just thought she was ordinary. Pretty in the face, but still ordinary. She had no idea what men were thinking when she walked by. Part of this had to do with her naivety, which stemmed from the fact that she was still a virgin.

Sarah was almost 30 now. She finished law school and began working as a Deputy District Attorney when she was only 24 years old. She was such an over-achiever that she had finished her undergraduate studies 1 year early. She was very young to have the accomplished career she had now. She was in her sixth year at the District Attorney's Office and was handling only the most serious felonies and high-profile cases. She had a history of winning the toughest trials. She was known for her sharp mind and her courtroom talent. She could use her femininity to reach the jury's emotions, and draw out their sympathies for the victims. She could do this just as easily as she could forcefully confront a criminal or defense witness in cross-examination like her toughest, most intimidating male counter-parts. It was her ability to transition between the masculine and the feminine at the appropriate time during trial that gave her the edge over many other lawyers in the courthouse. She was revered as an outstanding trial lawyer. And she prided herself in this accomplishment. She was actually addicted to it now. It was the reason she worked so hard, and sacrificed so much. All her childhood friends were married now and starting to have children. But Sarah had neglected that part of her life. She was too drawn into her career to notice that her 20s had passed by already. She was now almost 30, single and childless, without a potential boyfriend anywhere on the horizon. But her work was too consuming for her to appreciate the magnitude of what this meant. Her life was heading down a road that would leave her with nothing but her career if she didn't start making some changes soon.

This morning, Sarah put her hair up in a bun because she thought this was her most intimidating look. It reminded her of the mean old librarian who used to glare at her when she was in grade school. Sarah was a talkative and bubbly child who couldn't stay quiet in libraries. So she was constantly shushed with the meanest glares from the school librarian who always had her hair in a bun and her reading glasses hanging at the tip of her nose. The librarian would peer over the top of her glasses, give Sarah a scary glare and somehow yell the sound: "Shhsh!!!" Sarah knew that every kid had been shushed by a mean scary-looking librarian at one point in their childhood or another, and she used the same psychological ploy in her work today. She would use this trick when addressing police officers about their investigations, and she would use this trick when cross-examining defense witnesses she wanted to shake up so they wouldn't remember their stories correctly. If she could trip them up during their testimony, she could convince the jury they were lying.

Today, Sarah was cross-examining the defendant himself. Trial had closed yesterday at the end of the defendant's direct-examination, during which his own attorney asked him softball questions. Today was Sarah's opportunity to blow his story out of the water. So, after putting her hair up in the tightest, most intimidating bun she could wrap up, Sarah drew the chain of her reading glasses over her head. With the chain hanging around her neck and the glasses falling mid-way down her chest, Sarah picked up the glasses and put them on, at the very tip of her nose. She then leaned towards the mirror, peered over the top of her reading glasses, and practiced her favorite line. It was a question she used often. It was carefully worded so that she could alert the jury to an important point -- that the witness had just testified differently from what he had said before. In the mirror, Sarah glared over the top of her reading glasses, and with a stern, accusatory voice, she said: "Mr. Davis, that is *not* what you told police,..." Satisfied, that she had perfected her delivery of that line, Sarah turned away from the mirror and headed to work.

Sarah's morning was far different from David's. After leaving Lola's Bar, David and his friends went to a party in the Hollywood Hills. The party lasted until morning, but David left a few hours before dawn, with two women on his arm. One girl sat in the other's lap, in the passenger side of David's bright new yellow Lamborghini. The sports car was only meant for one driver and one passenger, but David was the type of man who needed two of the best looking passengers his lifestyle could attract, to share one seat. The women giggled and shrieked as David sped up to his own house in the Hollywood Hills, where the three of them had the kind of evening David had been missing during the weeks he'd been laid up. This morning, he woke up with his right arm sprawled out over Kandi's naked behind, and his left hand resting on Tisha's bare breast. He gave each handful a squeeze, and their private party began again.

David was a gentleman. He always took his overnight date to breakfast the next morning, even if there were two of them. So after his morning roll around with Kandi and Tisha, David called his home office in Beverly Hills and told his assistant to move his morning teleconference to the afternoon: "Tell them, I'm still wrapped up in a prior engagement and will need to delay the teleconference." Though his assistant was tempted to ask: "really, what's her name?" she didn't ask. She knew David well and knew he liked to be discreet. So she respected his privacy. David hung up his phone and caressed Kandi's legs, which were still wrapped around him. "Mmmm, wrapped up, huh? How do you like being wrapped like this?" she purred. "Mmmm, I love it," David hummed back. Tisha's breasts were pressed into his back, with her arms wrapped around his chest, "What about like this?" Tisha asked. He turned his head over his left shoulder, reaching his face back to give Tisha a kiss. "Mmm, I like that too."

David then decided he had enough energy left in him for a little more fun before breakfast, and the fun began again.

CHAPTER 3

White Sr., was an old man who would have retired by now if his son were worthy to take over his law firm. His son, White, Jr., had been out of law school seven years now but he still had not shown any signs of professional development. But White Sr., loved his son and was very proud of him. The day he graduated law school, even before he passed the bar exam, White Sr., had changed the name of his law firm from White & Smith, to White, White & Smith so as to proudly add his son's name to the name of his law firm. His partner, Jim Smith, was a good sport and had no objections to changing the name of the firm. He didn't have any sons of his own or any children who wanted to become law-yers, so he let Rick add his son to the name of the firm.

Each of them thought it was a good idea at the time. They thought it would show their clients that the firm was here to stay a long time and would be passed on from father to son and continue to deliver the high-est caliber legal performance they could find anywhere in the country.

But now, seven years later, the boy had turned out to be a disappoint-ment. He was not talented enough to handle a trial. His mind was not sharp enough to handle the complexities of the high profile white-collar crime cases the firm defended. He could only be given simple drug and prostitution cases, but even then, he would not be assigned to handle the trials. His work was limited to easy court appearances that even a court-certified law student could handle. White Jr., would handle arraignments, which were nothing more than hearings where the court would read the charges to the defendant, advise him of the maximum sentence, ask him how he wanted to plea, and decide how much the bail should be.

White Jr., also handled plea hearings and sentencing hearings, but only if a deal had been struck with the D.A.'s Office limiting their recommendation to a specific sentence. If the case involved "open-sentencing" where the court would hear arguments from both sides, White Jr., would not handle the hearing. As much as White Sr., loved his son, he had to acknowledge his son's shortcomings. He could not jeopardize the welfare of his clients, who trusted him to protect their liberty, only to favor his son the way men in other businesses had the luxury of doing.

White Sr., wondered if he was at fault for his son's failure to apply himself and develop his skills as an attorney. He wondered if maybe he spoiled the boy too much when he was growing up. He gave him the world and never made him work for it. Because White Sr., had grown up poor, he could not bear to tell his children "no" whenever they asked for something. Everything they wanted, they received without delay. White Sr., worked hard at everything he did, from putting himself through law school, to opening his own firm, to reaching the pinnacle of success and becoming a nationally recognized criminal defense attorney within his first five years of practice.

He had assumed that everyone in life would work this hard to achieve their goals. He had not factored into the equation, how spoiling a child from their youth could disrupt that motivation. Having grown up poor, he didn't know what being spoiled felt like and therefore, he was without the life experience to know what damage that could do to a child. So he gave his children everything - the best clothes, the coolest toys, luxury family vacations on every Christmas, Spring and Summer break.

He had given White, Jr., a red Ferrari as his first car, even before he had passed his driving test. He bought it for him and parked it outside their Beverly Hills mansion the night before White Jr.'s sixteenth birthday. He thought it would serve as incentive to pass the driver's test the next day. But White Jr. failed the driver's test three times.

Looking back on how he raised his children, White Sr., was filled with regret. He knew it was his fault they were spoiled. He knew it was his fault none of them were willing to work hard for anything. He continued to spoil them today, not knowing how to break the habit. Of course, it was too late now, anyhow. So they all had luxury cars, millions of dollars in their own bank accounts, and their own homes in Beverly Hills. If it was his fault they couldn't earn their own living, he had a duty to keep them in the comfort they grew up in.

Now White Sr., sat in the smoking lounge of his law firm and pondered the future of his firm with his partner Jim Smith. Each of them sat opposite each other in their own luxurious leather armchairs, divided by a coffee table. Jim Smith had his feet on the table, his ankles crossed as he leaned back and puffed on his cigar.

"Rick, this trial work is a young man's business."

"You've been saying that for 15 years, Jim."

"Then I'm 15 years too old for this. Why don't we just wrap it up Rick? It's been a good run. You and I started this place together our first year out of law school. We've amassed as much wealth as two old men could hope for. Our children are very comfortable, our wives are very comfortable. Why do we need to keep working this hard?"

"What do you mean, Jim? Just close up shop? Take our sign down, tell our clients, better luck with that law firm down the road?"

"That's exactly what I mean."

"We can't do that!"

"Why not?"

"I don't know. It just doesn't seem right."

"What's not right about it? We wouldn't be abandoning anyone. We would slowly wind down the firm. Finish up our current cases, not take any new ones. Then one day, like it's summer break, our final day in court will come, and we go on and live the rest of our lives traveling the world with our wives, golfing, gardening, going to Disney Land. Anything. Anything but this. Anything but slaving away night after night, preparing for another long and grueling trial. What's not right about that, Rick?"

Rick thought long and hard about what seemed so wrong with the idea of closing down this institution he had worked so hard to build. He furrowed his brow, took a long puff of his cigar, blow the smoke out slowly, then the answer came to him.

"I want to leave a legacy, Jim."

"Ack! Legacy! That's so egotistical and over-rated. I think I'd rather enjoy my retirement, and not wait until I die for my legacy to finally come in and promise to continue my firm name into perpetuity."

Rick looked at his old friend and wondered how he could just walk away so easily. Then it dawned on him. Jim only had daughters. He didn't understand the need to pass your legacy on to your son. But Rick tried to make Jim understand.

"Think about your daughter, the artist. Are you proud of her paintings?"

"Why yes, of course!"

"Would you want her paintings to remain on museum walls for as long as Picasso's paintings have?"

Jim Smith smiled brightly at the thought of his daughter's artwork becoming so great, and he said: "Sure, now I understand what you mean."

"Then will you wait this thing out with me? I have the perfect young woman in mind who could be the future of our firm."

"Ah, yes, you're darling Sarah. She is quite a little whipper snapper!"

"Jim, she beat me in court the other day! Can you believe it? She was amazing! Only God-given talent can make a lawyer as great as Sarah! There are men in that D.A.'s Office who are 20 years her senior who have never won a case against me! She had the jury eating out of the palm of her hand."

The image of great trial work made Jim's face light up. He was as addicted to the thrill of this business as his old friend Rick was. Though he talked about it, he never really believed he was ready for retirement. The thrill of the fight was too intoxicating. As Jim began to picture Sarah leading his firm into the future, another thought popped into his mind.

"Wouldn't they be a cute couple, Sarah and White, Jr."

"I've often thought that myself, Jim. I've thought, if only my son could court that girl and sweep her off her feet, she could be the 'White' that replaces me as I pass the torch on to her and my son."

"That's sweet, Rick. I hope to congratulate you at their wedding one day."

CHAPTER 4

White Jr., watched Sarah walk up the stairs. It was a rare sight to see her in a dress. It was an even more rare sight to see her without her typical, slightly over-sized suit jacket that she always used to hide her body. So, he stopped and enjoyed the view. He didn't get to see those curves very often. White Jr., believed Sarah hid her beautiful body from men on purpose. He thought it was her way of being mean to all men, trying to prove she would always have the upper hand, the way she was always so ruthless and unforgiving in the courtroom, arguing for convictions and harsh sentences. He resented her for that, but even that resentment was not enough to quiet his desire for her. It actually made her more alluring, more enticing.

It was hot outside and she must have been coming back from lunch. Her thick, long dark hair, which she hardly ever wore down, fell free today. It clung to her face, as if she had slightly perspired on her walk back from lunch. It looked so sexy. For the briefest moment, White Jr., thought of Sarah sweaty and naked in his bedroom. It was a fantasy that crossed his mind on more than one occasion. But as much as he fantasized about her, he also hated her. He had made his attempts to court her two years ago. He gave it a real good try, but she never seemed interested. In fact, she didn't even seem to notice he was courting her. He would buy her a coffee, ask her to join him for lunch, and invite her to drinks. Sometimes she would accept the coffee or the lunch, but she would never accept the drink invitations. At lunch or coffee, she never brought down her professional barrier, no matter how much he flattered her, complimented her and delivered lines that made all other women putty in his hands.

White Jr., was very good looking. He was blonde, with well-tanned skin and all American good looks. He was tall and lean, with defined arms, shoulders and abs. He looked great on the beach and spent a lot of time there, because he never worked very hard. He was always popular with women. In his high school days, he was the most popular guy in school. In college and law school he was considered the most eligible bachelor -- but it was all his father's hard work that gave him that status. White Jr., took it all for granted. The luxury cars, the money, the status -- none of it was earned, it was all handed down to him. White Jr., was born into the lifestyle. He had no idea how his father struggled and worked so hard to become the legend that he was, and to provide his family with the luxury and ease of living that White Jr., took for granted. White Jr., loved his father and looked up to him as an icon. He yearned for his respect but never understood that it was his lack of ambition and drive that would always prevent him from fully gaining his father's respect.

Growing up in Southern California, White Jr., had too many distractions entertaining him to be able to work as hard as his father. There were girls, there were parties, there were waves to ride. He always got to the office late, and left early because he would spend his mornings and his afternoons surfing. He never handled any cases that involved anything more complicated than an arraignment in a misdemeanor case, or a plea and sentencing hearing with an agreed-upon sentence. He would only handle the kind of hearing that required no preparation. Everything that came to White Jr., in life, came easy. So he saw no need to apply himself.

Because of his good looks and his father's money, girls came very easy to White Jr.; so, when he couldn't peak Sarah's interest, it frustrated him. It bruised his ego and made him a little angry with her. At first, he thought it was a thrilling challenge. But later, he just became pissed off about it. It was even more frustrating that his father kept dropping obvious hints, that he thought White, Jr., should court Sarah. He would often say things like, "Son, you would make your mother and I very proud of you, if you brought home a woman like Sarah." He would go on about how a man needed to marry an intelligent woman, someone who could be his equal, someone who could contribute to his success. "Maybe a lawyer, like yourself!" he would say. And it always circled back to Sarah. His father couldn't have a discussion with him about settling down with the right woman, without mentioning Sarah as the example of the woman White Jr., was expected to marry. White Jr., would never tell his father that he had already tried, but she rejected him. Instead, White Jr., would say, "I prefer blondes." His father's lectures only added to the pressure and the frustration of not being able to crack Sarah's shell. It made him feel like he had something to prove. He wanted to prove he could get Sarah.

It was slowly becoming an obsession. He had to stop dating brunettes because he accidentally called his last brunette girlfriend "Sarah" when they were in bed together. She went ape-shit. She started screaming at him and throwing things at him. She broke his bedroom window throwing a golf ball at him. He had ducked just in the nick of time only to hear it crashing through the window behind him. After that experience, he decided that it was not safe to date brunettes anymore. He had also decided after that occasion, that he should make another attempt at Sarah. So, in his next attempt, he was more direct. He convinced her to come to dinner with him so that it would be a more romantic setting. But when he reached across the table for her hand, she jerked it away quickly. Attempting to ease her into comfort, White Jr., had smoothly said: "Sarah, don't be shy." Sarah quickly snapped back: "I'm not shy, I just don't mix business with pleasure. Please do not do that again." Her sharp response left him feeling like she was such a cold-hearted bitch.

His feelings of animosity grew after he heard snickering in the courthouse about how a talented trial lawyer like her could not date a man who never tried a case. Though White Jr., was a stud and an eligible bachelor outside the courthouse walls, in the courthouse he was considered the disappointment who could never measure up to his father, the legend. He had assumed that Sarah was telling everyone about his advance and that she was laughing behind his back about it. However, Sarah never mentioned his advances to anyone, as she would never want to embarrass him. A group of their colleagues were dining in the restaurant the day he reached for her hand. They all saw how quickly she yanked it out of his reach. And the rumors and the laughing spread throughout the courthouse like wild fire among the younger generation of attorneys. But because Sarah was the subject of the rumor, she had never heard it. She was completely unaware of White Jr.'s animosity or the cause of it. She continued to maintain her professionalism with him as if nothing had ever happened.

Today, the sight of Sarah's curves reignited White Jr.'s desires -- which flared his hate for her along with his desire for her. He stood at the top of the stairs until she reached him, and he began walking alongside her.

"Just get back from lunch?"

"Yes."

"It's a hot day, isn't it."

"Really hot."

"Kind of like you, Sarah."

She stopped walking and looked at him. "What?"

"Nothing, I was just teasing."

"Richard, I thought we went over this a few years ago."

"Relax," he said. "It was just a joke. And a compliment, I might add. You should learn how to accept those."

Sarah's face softened when he said that, and the hint of a smile curved at the corner of her lips. White Jr., hoped that was a green light. So he lifted his finger and gently pushed her hair off her face to tuck it behind her ear. Sarah jerked backwards quickly and instinctively swatted at his hand. "Don't!" she snapped, as she turned and quickly walked away from him. She didn't mean to be rude but the sudden intimate gesture caught her off guard and she didn't like it. It was a knee-jerk reaction to the discomfort she felt. But White Jr., was not used to being rejected by women. Anger flashed in his eyes, and desire turned to pure hate, as he glared at Sarah while she walked away from him. He glared at her until she was around the corner and out of sight, her high heels clunking hard on the ground, as if taunting him with the sound of her leaving. His mind was filled with anger, as he blamed her for all the inadequacies he felt about his career, his poor standing in the legal community, and the disappointment he knew his father felt about him.

White Jr., was wrong about Sarah. She was not a stingy man-hating feminist who intentionally hid her body from men to punish or deprive them. In fact, she had no idea that men loved her body. It was simply her nature to dress conservatively, largely because she was still a virgin and a little uncomfortable with the idea of being sexy; but also because she was an attorney, and she believed that only the utmost professionalism should be presented in her demeanor and attire. This meant covering her large breasts so that they were not so noticeable. The best way to do that was with a slightly over-sized suit jacket that was large enough to cover her breasts, which meant it completely swallowed her curves and made her look wider and less attractive than she really was.

Also, Sarah was not a cold-hearted bitch. Quite the contrary, Sarah had a very soft heart. She never wanted to hurt anyone's feelings. Usually, she chose her words wisely so as to avoid accidentally hurting anyone. The only time she lost this trait was when someone caught her off guard and pushed her past her comfort zone, which would cause an instant-reaction that appeared to be a cold, but unintentional rejection, as she would reach to enforce her boundaries.

It was Sarah's soft heart that made her work so hard at her job. Her ruthless, unforgiving zeal for punishing criminals was driven by her passion for protecting the innocent. Sarah remembered the faces of every victim in the cases she prosecuted. She remembered the five children she saved from a stepmother who moved in shortly after their mother died and began severely abusing them. She remembered the defendant's ex-husband who had lost his battle in divorce court over custody of the woman's biological children, years before the report of child-abuse against the stepchildren arose. Sarah remembered the look of relief, releasing years of worry, on the ex-husband's face when Sarah obtained a restraining order pre-trial, which allowed his own children to return to his home where it was safe. She remembered how he and his new wife couldn't express their gratitude enough as they thanked her, and thanked her for finally bringing that evil woman to justice.

"No one believed us," they had said. "It is so hard for a father to prove the mother is unfit. Everyone thought we made up the allegations just to get an edge in the divorce case, but she was abusing our children too. We're so glad you caught her and you are finally stopping her."

It was this gratitude and the ability to give crime victims safety that gave Sarah all the reward she needed to keep working hard, for very little pay. Money could never match this reward. Sarah also remembered the faces of the retired couples who had lost their life savings to a con artist.

She remembered how they cried after Sarah led an investigation which located the stolen money and returned it to the victims. It was the memory of these faces that kept Sarah at the office late at night making sure she had an ironclad case that would bring wrongdoers to justice and provide their victims with the protection they needed. It was these stories that led Sarah to sacrifice her own happiness by forgetting to develop her social life as she slaved away, long nights and every weekend developing a rock solid case, every time. The victims in her cases, and the people who were still out there, yet to become one of her case files, were the reason she would always reject White Sr.'s job offers that could have instantly made her wealthy, by simply accepting the job. She sacrificed it all because of her soft heart.

Tonight, Sarah was still at the office around 11:00 p.m. She hadn't eaten since lunch because she was too pre-occupied with a complicated white-collar crime case that the police were building against a man who had fooled the members of his church into contributing to a false charity. As she reviewed the file with stern concentration, Sarah's cell phone rang, and she answered:

"Hi Mom."

"Hi sweetie, how are you?"

"Good," Sarah said absent-mindedly as she continued reviewing the evidence the police had gathered.

"You sound distracted, are you still at the office?"

"Yes Mom."

"Don't you get scared staying there so late at night?"

"Mom, this place is safer than my apartment, the police are always patrolling around this building, criminals aren't stupid enough to linger around here."

"But what if there's one that hates you? They'll know what building you're in, what if they wait while you walk to your car?"

"Mom, it's fine. I'll be safe. I'll have an officer walk me to my car."

Sarah heard her mother sigh, as she moved on to the next topic her mother harassed Sarah about every night. The conversation about this topic was nearly identical each time:

"What did you eat today?"

"I don't know."

"You don't know! How can you not know?

"I forgot."

"You forgot, that means you didn't eat! You need to eat, Sarah, you need to take care of yourself."

"I know, Mom, I will."

"You will? You always say you will, but you never do."

"Tomorrow, I will. I promise."

Sarah's mother then changed the topic to the next thing she frequently nagged Sarah about.

"What are you doing this weekend?"

"I have a lot of work to do, but don't worry, I'll do it from home."

"More work? How are you supposed to meet someone and start a family if all you do is work?"

"I don't know, Mom. When the time is right, the right man will come find me."

"You need to go to church, Sarah. That's where you'll meet a nice man."

Sarah smiled at the irony of her mother's words, as she looked down at her file where a man had used that very logic to swindle the people who went to his church. All the victims said they never would have imagined he would do such a thing. "He never misses church. He is here every Sunday," each one of the victims had said. But Sarah didn't tell her mom that story. She did not want to burden her mother with the ugliness of life outside their small town. She wanted to let her believe that there was one safe place a person could always go and be surrounded by good people. Besides, the town her mother and father still lived in was one where families knew each other for generations. Everyone knew who was trustworthy and who was not. There was almost no risk that the same thing could happen to Sarah's mother. So, she didn't need to be warned about such dangers. Instead of using this case to argue with her mother, Sarah said:

"Ok, Mom. I'll go to church on Sunday."

"Thank you, Sarah," her mother sighed with relief. "And make sure you get involved in a church group doing community service, that's how you'll get to know more people and expand your social circle. And, if you're working on a community service project, you won't have to feel guilty that you're not doing your work."

"That's a good idea mom. I'll do that."

"I love you, honey. Good night."

"I love you too, Mom. Good night."

The following Sunday, Sarah did as she had promised her mother. She went to church. The priest gave a sermon about the importance of family and serving the most important role God intended for us all -- which was to find our soul mates, whom he had chosen for us, and create a family that we were to raise with the high integrity and morals that would always lead them down God's path and enable them to make the right choices as adults when their parents were no longer able to make decisions for them.

Sarah believed in everything the priest was saying that day. Her belief in his words left her with a heavy burden. She now felt the immensity of the pressure to find someone before it was too late to start her own family. Loneliness started to descend upon Sarah. She couldn't figure out how to break the cycle of working so hard. She didn't know how she would ever be able to find the time to get to know someone well enough to be able to decide to spend the rest of her life with him. She also felt like the role she played in the District Attorney's Office was just as, if not more, important than the role the priest described. Sarah pondered that thought. Were there some people God created to live without a soul mate so that they could put all their energy into protecting the innocent? Sarah wondered about this a lot. She used it as her justification to continue her workaholic behavior. Ultimately, she decided to take solace in the fact that if she were meant to marry, God would send her the right man, and it would just happen.

CHAPTER 5

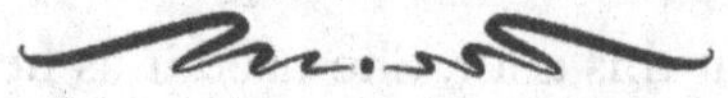

David loved having threesomes, but he usually hated the morning after. In the morning, the thrill of last night's party was gone. The alcohol had worn off, and the women were now showing their true colors. These two were nothing like Tisha and Kandi, who were best friends that enjoyed sharing. These two were warring females who played the games rich guys like to play just so that they could get close to them. These two were strategists. The strategy of a woman like this was to try to convince the man that she was all the fun he could hope for; and therefore, he shouldn't be afraid of settling down with her. She presented herself as a good-time party girl, but secretly planned on landing the man.

Today, each girl was practically shoving the other one out of the way so that only she could be close to David. David hated that. The ugliness of that jealous behavior always killed the joy of having two women in his bed. When the blonde went to the restroom, the brunette started telling David all the bad things she could think to say about the blonde. The brunette carried on:

"She's nothing like me. She'll fuck your best friend. But I'm not like that. I'm here because I really care about you, and I'm open-minded enough to explore all your sexual desires. I only share you because I know you like it. But if you wanted an exclusive relationship, I would be soooo happy. I would never pressure you though. I'm just saying, that I will be exclusive with you and whatever you like, I'll go along with. But if you want to keep having threesomes, I'd rather we be with a different girl each time, so that our connection remains constant, and we don't get confused about each other's feelings."

David rubbed his forehead as the brunette chattered on. Finally, he interrupted her: "I have headache, please excuse me."

Today, David couldn't handle the warring females. They had been bickering all morning and talking trash about each other at every opportunity. It was David's custom to always have breakfast with the women he bedded the night before. He did this because he never wanted to feel like a sleaze bag who used women. He liked to think that spending an evening with one or more women was simply mutual fun between consenting adults who enjoyed each other's company. He thought morning breakfast with your date (or dates) from the night before was quality time spent together, and therefore, the night before couldn't be considered a cheap and sleazy one-night stand. But today, the bickering between the women was ruining that philosophy. Although David hated having to divert from his customary morning-after breakfast, today he just couldn't go through with it. So, David walked the two women downstairs and asked them to make themselves comfortable. "Ladies, my butler will see to it that you are driven home safely, after the chef prepares whatever gourmet breakfast you would like to enjoy before you are driven home. My apologies, but I cannot join you for breakfast, I have very important business that awaits."

David then drove off in his black Mercedes. He rarely drove this car, but today, he felt like a less flashy car than his usual yellow Lamborghini. As he drove away, David instructed his voice-automated system to dial Frank.

"Hey, Frank, meet me at Bouchon for breakfast."

"Breakfast? I thought you would still be with your 'company' this morning."

"No, the 'company' was giving me a headache. I need a quiet breakfast, just the guys."

At that, Frank laughed out loud. "Ok buddy, I'll be there."

At breakfast, David asked Frank, "So where is a guy supposed to find a nice girl to settle down with?"

Frank answered, "Not in Hollywood, buddy. And I can assure you, 'nice girls' don't have threesomes."

"But..."

"No David. They don't have threesomes."

"That's just a sexual preference, Frank. It doesn't mean she's not a good person. The same as being gay is a sexual preference. We don't deny gay people rights because of their sexual preference, do we? We let them participate in politics. We let them adopt children. Society allows this because we don't judge a person's character based on their sexual preference, right?"

"Wrong. Gay people have also fought hard for the right to get married -- that is a monogamous relationship. It involves only 2 people, not 3. You need to be honest with yourself David. A girl who is willing to watch you put your finger in another girl's pussy while you're kissing her breasts is not a girl who loves you. You have to get that straight."

"I guess that makes sense. It's just a hard habit to break. Do you know how nice it is to not have to limit yourself to just one?"

"Yes, I'm sure that's very nice. But if you're talking about settling down, you need to readjust your habits. It's like when you left Wall Street and came to Hollywood. The stock exchange required a much different lifestyle and work method than the movie business does. In New York, you had to be at work around the same time you are just barely leaving last night's party in Hollywood, right?"

"Right."

"So, if you really are ready to settle down with a nice girl, you have to change your life again. You have to start going to places nice girls go."

"Ok. Now tell me where that is. I only know where wannabe actresses willing to have threesomes go. Who else is out there? And where do they spend their time?"

"I hate to break this to you, but they hang out at the same types of parties your step-father would go to. They are professional women, with conservative lifestyles. They go to doctor, lawyer, or accountant networking events."

"Oh god! Are you serious!"

"Yes. And I know of one that is happening tonight. You should come with me. It's at the Montage. A poker buddy of mine is a big-name white-collar defense attorney. He's throwing a party for his colleagues and he invited me. You should come."

"Fine. I'll try it. This morning, I was just beginning to think three-somes aren't worth the trouble anymore. So, you've caught me on a good day. I'm willing to go to an event full of boring people now."

Frank slapped David on the back, cordially and laughed. "Don't think of them as boring. Just think of them as women who secure their clothing with more complicated locks. It could be a new challenge for you. How do I get a lawyer out of her suit?"

David then smiled. "Yeah, I like the sound of that challenge!"

CHAPTER 6

It was Friday night and Sarah had left the office early. She was getting ready for a party that White Sr., had invited her to. He was known for throwing an elegant party at a fancy place every few months. He always invited Sarah. These parties were mostly filled with defense lawyers. A very select few of White Sr.'s favorite prosecutors were invited as well. Besides herself, the only other prosecutors that were invited were personal friends of White Sr., whom he had known since law school.

Sarah knew this was all part of White Sr.'s attempt to lure her over to working at his firm. But she enjoyed these parties, so she went to them even though she was still very committed to remaining a Deputy District Attorney. The parties would also include other non-lawyer guests that White Sr., knew outside the practice of law. There would be the occasional poker buddy who could be anywhere from his son's age to his own age. There would be his golf buddies. There would be people from the various country clubs he was a member of, and their wives. There would be his friends from college. It was usually a good crowd and a fun party. Elegant, and respectable, but still fun.

Today, the party was going to be at the Montage Hotel in Beverly Hills. White Sr., had reserved an entire bar inside the hotel for his private party. Sarah had never been there before but she was told she could find it easily. The bar was called Parq and it was located on the side of the hotel along an actual park. She was told to look for the two valet umbrellas out in front of the actual park, next to the grand hotel. She could park in the valet and enter directly into the bar from the side entrance without having to come through the hotel lobby.

As Sarah began to dress for the party, she selected a dark navy blue dress she had never worn before. It was part of a dress suit, but she was not going to wear the matching coat. Although she wanted to look appropriately professional, she did not want to look as if she were dressed for court. She had never worn the dress to work because it was a little too tight to wear to the office, but was acceptable for a party. Although the style was meant to be conservative, it hugged Sarah's curves so tightly, that on her body, it looked very sexy. The sleeves were a tank-style and the v-neck plunged low enough to reveal her cleavage. The dress was cinched in tight at the waist and accentuated her hourglass figure. It was so tight around her large breasts that she had to lift them to make room to fit them into the dress. The dress was tight enough that her boobs remained propped up as if she wore a corset. She had to allow her breasts to protrude slightly out of the v-neck so the top of the dress could zip up. The dress hugged her waist and her hips tightly and narrowed at the knees. It was perfectly shaped as if it had been drawn to follow every curve of Sarah's body.

It was a very rare occasion that Sarah would allow this much sex appeal to show in front of her colleagues; but it was the end of the week and she was ready to let her hair down and feel like a woman. She was even going to allow herself to indulge in a little Tequila tonight. She knew to avoid Tequila because she believed the drink to be a love potion. It always made her feel flirty and amorous. Sometimes, one sip of a Tequila beverage would awaken the senses between her legs. She knew it was dangerous for a virgin to drink Tequila, so it was not often that she permitted herself that indulgence. But tonight, Sarah needed a release. Her workweek had been a long week of heated courtroom confrontations that required her to fight aggressively, like a man. She needed to reconnect with her femininity tonight. Dressing sexy for a party and drinking Tequila was the quickest way to do that. But she would only have a little because she needed to preserve her respectable reputation.

Sarah pulled up to the valet in front of the park and immediately recognized her colleagues gathered by the side entrance of the building. Many of the familiar guests at the party were collected outside the bar on an elegant tiled patio. The patio was covered with beautiful architecture containing arches and columns one would see in a painting depicting the Roman Empire during the height of its glory. Sarah greeted her colleagues on the patio then entered Parq in search of the host.

More elegance awaited her inside. The room was somehow cozy, luxurious and elegant all at once. The warm earth tone colors and grand fire place made it feel as comfortable as a private living room, but the six giant chandeliers hanging along the ceiling, and the gorgeous architecture creating the illusion of sections separated by archways reminded guests that this was the sort of luxury typically found only in a 5 diamond hotel. Larger than life oil paintings so high in quality that they appeared to be painted in 3d decorated the walls. They were so magnificent, they could have easily been mistaken for something a person could find at the Louvre in France. The furniture was elegant but cozy. Sofas and sofa-chairs with coffee tables gave guests a very comfortable place to relax. The dining tables were low enough to compliment the relaxed but elegant decor of the sofas. Each table was surrounded by armchairs, and was decorated only with fine china, real silver and linen napkins. Even the cocktail napkins were linen.

Sarah took in the beauty of the place and smiled at the thought of what a class act White Sr., truly was. He worked hard for his wealth and he enjoyed it too. He was kind and generous enough to invite his colleagues and friends to enjoy it with him at these private parties he threw every few months. Sarah considered herself lucky to be respected by him. She made her way through the crowd until she found White Sr.

"Sarah, my dear! There you are! I'm so glad you could make it!"

"You know I wouldn't miss this," she smiled warmly.

White Sr., greeted her with a hug and introduced her to his friends.

"Gentlemen, let me introduce you to my other heir. She is not my real daughter but she is like a daughter to me. This is my successor in interest. She is the most talented young trial attorney you will find anywhere in America!"

Sarah laughed. She did not argue with him because these were his friends and this was his night. "Oh Mr. White, you are far too kind."

"Is she one of your attorneys, Rick?" his friend from college asked.

"Not yet. I'm letting her practice and refine her skills at the expense of the government, serving in the District Attorney's Office, until she finally sees the light and comes to work for me!"

His group of friends erupted with laughter. Only White Sr., could so proudly declare that a prosecutor, a rival, was his protégé, and heir to his throne.

White Sr., had had enough to drink already, that he hadn't thought about the effect of his words. He only meant to flatter Sarah and entertain his friends. He had not considered how his words reflected on his own son. But that part was not lost on White Jr. White Jr., stood outside the circle of his father and his father's old friends from college, as if he were an outcast. He heard everything his father said about Sarah and it enraged him. That was his father, not hers! It was his name on the firm's door, not hers! His father should have told his friends how proud he was of him, not her! His father's friends should have been surrounding him, inquiring about him, patting him on the back and recognizing him as his father's pride and joy. But instead, it was Sarah who was receiving that attention.

White Jr., had too much love and respect for his father to hate him. So instead, all his pain, all his rage, all his anger was directed at Sarah -- the woman who stole his father's attention. The woman who stole his father's respect. The woman who out-performed him professionally. The woman who was going to steal the family business that was meant for him! White Jr., hated Sarah with every cell in his body. He looked at her with pure hate and rage. He hated how attractive she looked tonight, as if she were there only to taunt and tease him. The woman who rejected him two years ago. The woman he could never have was now elevating herself above him, even in his father's eyes.

The stronger his physical attraction for her grew, the more he hated her. Now, she decides to dress sexy!? While at a party to be shown off in front of his father's friends. The so-called "perfect woman?" The talented, smart and attractive heir his father wished he had? The memory of Sarah's rejection of him two years ago, now mixed with his hate for her stealing his father's attention and respect. It made him sick to his stomach. He had to get out of there. He slammed his drink down so hard, it startled the bartender. He stormed out of Parq with such anger he almost knocked over a waitress. He continued without apologizing. When he reached the valet stand, he cussed at the valet driver. "Get me my fucking car, now! You incompetent imbecile!" When they brought him his car, White Jr., squealed the tires of his red Ferrari, peeling out and driving off in anger.

But the party was loud and lively and nobody but the staff noticed White Jr.'s temper tantrum. Sarah continued to mingle with guests and enjoy the party. She had no idea that White Sr.'s son hated her so badly.

David pulled into the valet at the Montage hotel in Beverly Hills. The valet driver didn't give him a ticket because they all knew David. They would always park his car out front because flashy, luxury cars like the one David drove served to adorn the building and maintain its reputation as a luxury hotel serving the finest guests. David loved the spa and the restaurants at that hotel, so he had an account there. He frequented the place and all the staff knew his name.

David entered the lobby of the beautifully appointed hotel and walked down the hall towards a charming little bar called Parq, where Frank had told him the private party would be. As David entered Parq from the hallway, he stopped at the Maître D's podium. What he saw made his heart stop. The sensation hit him so hard, he had to grab onto the podium with one hand to steady himself. He tried to catch his breath. He had never seen such a beauty before. She was radiant. She was elegant. She was poised. She stood with strength and confidence, but she was oh so feminine. That body. Those curves. That long shiny black hair, falling down her shoulders, landing at breast level, gently wrapping around each breast, as if to tease his eyes. David couldn't speak. He was breathless. This dark-haired beauty did things to him. She made his heart skip a few beats. She stirred him inside, in a way that no one else had. He felt a strong desire for her that was coming more from his heart than from his groin. There was softness in her brown eyes, and an innocence in her face that made David want to protect her. This woman captured David's heart. It was love at first sight. David took one look at Sarah, and knew, right then and there, that she was to be his wife.

His heart began to race, almost as if panic was rising within him. He needed to collect himself. He stood at the Maître D's podium, just watching her for a little while. She was standing at a table where only men were seated, most of them older with gray hair. They all wore business suits and appeared to be accomplished businessmen. The men were looking up at Sarah and seemed to be mesmerized by her. David noticed however, that they were not ogling her. They seemed to not even notice her luscious curves. Instead, they were looking up at her face as she addressed them. These men respected her. She commanded respect in her demeanor, and they all gave it to her. When Sarah finished her story, the men all roared with laughter. David heard one of them say, "That happened to me once! I was in Judge Johnson's courtroom, and..."

Lawyers. Of course, they were lawyers, this was a lawyers' party. David then realized that what he had been observing was a group of lawyers telling courtroom war stories. And the black-haired beauty that stole his heart, was one of them. She was a lawyer.

David's mind flashed to the conversation he had with Frank that morning. This was the type of woman Frank was talking about - a professional woman whose clothes were secured by a more complicated lock. David knew, with just one look at her, that Sarah's lock would be extra complicated. But he also knew, the combination to the lock that would release her clothing would be encrypted on the key to her heart. David needed the key to her heart. He wanted the key to her heart. It was the only way to take care of his. This woman was special.

Just then, David heard Sarah say: "Gentlemen, it's been a lovely evening. Mr. White has out done himself again. I look forward to seeing you all at his next soirée."

Oh no! She was saying goodbye! David realized the dark-haired beauty was saying goodbye. And she was at the other end of the room, near the other exit. He had to reach her! David began walking quickly towards her but there were at least 200 people in that small room, and it was difficult to get around them. He kept his eye on his target as he made his way through the crowd, then Frank stepped in front of him. "David! You made it!"

Frank put his arm around David's shoulder, "It's great to see you, Buddy! Let me introduce you to ..."

"Frank, I have to go."

"Where? You just got here?"

"This is important Frank, let me get by, I'll explain later."

David then broke free of Frank and hurried past the crowd. Sarah had exited already. He could see her through the window waiting at the valet stand. He had to reach her in time!

CHAPTER 7

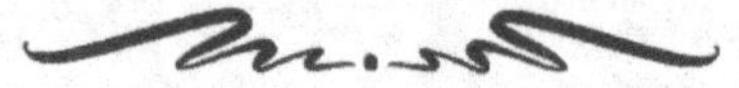

David was on his back, looking up. He watched her tilt her head back in ecstasy, her long black hair falling down her naked skin, caressing her breasts, as her body rocked with pleasure on top of his manhood. David couldn't believe it. The black-haired beauty from last night, was in his bed. He thrust his groin upwards to give her even more pleasure. She threw her head back, shouting even louder. She began to rock him harder and faster, screaming "oooh, ooohh...." David loved this moment. But he hated himself. What was he doing!? He was supposed to get to know her. He was supposed to love her and protect her. He was supposed to make her his wife. This was not the path to a long-lasting relationship. He couldn't even remember how he had gotten the black-haired beauty into his bed last night. David was confused. But he was too immersed in the pleasure of the experience to bother making any sense of what was going on. So he thrust upward again and tilted his own head back in ecstasy.

Then suddenly, his alarm rang. Loudly. It startled him. He sat straight up in his bed, alone. What!? David looked around the room. He felt around in his bed frantically, as if trying to find something that was lost. Where was she?! As David's mind cleared out of the slumber of sleep, he realized: he had been dreaming. The dark-haired beauty did not come home with him last night. He had barely made it to the valet stand in time to watch her slip into her car and drive off. Damn it! Damn it! He was so frustrated now. Still erect from his erotic dream, and angry about having lost the woman of his dreams without even having had the opportunity to speak to her, the frustration was unbearable. David yanked the covers off him and threw them hard to the side. He then headed for the shower. A cold shower.

Last night, David had been so disappointed when that dark-haired beauty had slipped away from him, that he couldn't go back in to the party. He walked along the sidewalk towards the front of the building where he had left his car with the hotel's valet. He got into his car and left without saying bye to Frank. He drove home to his mansion in Malibu because he wanted a longer drive to allow the thoughts that were swirling around in his mind to roam. He also needed to be in his sanctuary. He was surprised by how deeply disappointed he could feel at the loss of a woman he'd only seen and never spoken to. The sadness and disappointment was so overwhelming that he needed to retreat to his sanctuary. When he got home and climbed into bed, David had fallen asleep yearning to hold that black-haired beauty in his arms. He figured that was the reason he woke up to that erotic dream of her this morning. The dream was so vivid and it felt so real! This woman kept occupying David's mind, today.

After his cold shower, David took his coffee onto the upper balcony. He loved being in front of the ocean. The feel of the waves rolling towards him always put him at ease. The air was warm this morning and the waves were loud. It was calming. David put his cup down and walked over to the railing. Grabbing on with both hands he leaned into the wind so as to feel a little closer to the ocean. This is the spot David sent out all his prayers. He always felt closest to God in front of the ocean. And today, he prayed with all his heart and all of his soul, that God would bring that woman back to him, very soon. He stared out at the powerful crashing waves as he imagined Sarah walking towards him with a warm smile. He thought of what he would say to her. He thought of what she would say to him. And his heart warmed with a smile that shined in his face.

Sarah was on the beach in Santa Monica. She sat on the sand as close to the water as she could sit without getting wet. She watched the waves roll towards her. Sarah came to the beach every Saturday and Sunday morning. Sitting in front of the ocean was like pressing the "reset" button for Sarah. This was the only place that allowed her to release the heavy burden she carried in her work. The waves always washed away her stress. With each wave that rolled towards her this morning, Sarah felt more and more relaxed. Then, one wave, much larger and more powerful than all the rest, suddenly crashed in front of her. This wave brought Sarah a different emotion. As the wave came rolling towards her with great power, Sarah felt like it carried a strong love with it. As it crashed in front of her, she felt as if the love of a man had entered her heart, brought from somewhere out in the ocean. She did not have an image in her mind of what the man looked like or who he was. She just had an overwhelming feeling that someone out there loved her. It reminded her of that disembodied feeling she felt walking into Lola's bar, which gave her a yearning for someone she didn't know.

Sarah had no idea that David was standing on his balcony in Malibu, in that very moment, sending his love for her out across the ocean. She couldn't visualize him because she didn't see him last night. She had no idea what he was going through this morning. Sarah stared at the ocean, a little confused by her emotions. Unable to make sense of it, she dismissed the feeling again, the same way she had dismissed the feeling at Lola's bar. She decided these emotions were the result of a more general feeling of loneliness caused by the lack of a proper social life. She decided to rollerblade to Venice Beach, along the boardwalk where it would be bustling with people. She knew this great place that served imported beer and would stop in there. It was properly named, "On the Waterfront Cafe." Still sitting in front of the ocean, Sarah used the voice-command to send a text to her friend Cynthia. Looking out onto the great Pacific Ocean, Sarah said out loud: "Meet me at On the Waterfront Cafe in Venice Beach."

David was now sitting in his favorite armchair on his upper balcony sipping his coffee. One of the movies he invested in had finished filming and he was supposed to be getting ready to go to a wrap party at the Roosevelt Hotel. But he didn't want to today. Something about staring out into the ocean suddenly gave him an urgent desire to spend the day in Venice. It was a warm day, perfect for a cold beer at that place that serves beer imported from Germany with a name he can't pronounce. He would just point at it on the menu. It was the beer everyone there was drinking. He began to text Frank: "Meet me at that Waterfront Cafe place in ..." But before he could finish, his phone rang in his hands. It was his assistant. "Where should I send the limo to pick you up?"

"Don't send it. I'm not going."

"But you can't miss this party."

"Why not?"

"Remember, you said big important names were going to be there today, and I was supposed to remind you, you couldn't miss this party. You said you needed to be there to make connections to discuss that major project you were asked to invest in. You said you needed to pick their brains to help you feel out whether or not the opportunity would bring you a huge gain or a disastrous loss."

"Oh shit. You're right. I forgot. Send the limo to Malibu."

David was sulking in the back of his limo like a little boy who was told he couldn't go outside and play. He wanted to be in Venice Beach. He didn't want to have to go into Hollywood for work. He felt irritated and grumpy. So he helped himself to the fully stocked bar that his limo driver always kept ready to serve. As he picked up the tumbler and filled it with ice cubes, he made a note in his mind to give the limo driver a raise. As he poured the Jack Daniels, he also made a note to give his assistant a raise. She did exactly what she was supposed to do today. She kept him on track. David took a sip of his Jack and Coke and relaxed in the back of his limo. He had to get himself in a good mood quick so he could do his thing at this party.

Sarah was roller-blading to Venice, her hips swinging seductively as she moved. Her long hair was blowing in the wind and her smile was as bright as the sun. It was a warm summer day, and she was dressed for the occasion. She wore a skimpy little string bikini covered only by a very small short pink swimsuit-skirt, which did not fully cover the bottom. She ignored all the men who hooted, hollered, and catcalled her as she glided by. She just smiled and kept gliding on.

She thought it was funny how men reacted to a woman in a bikini, even if she was overweight. But what Sarah did not realize, is that she was not overweight. She was too naive to understand that her naturally large curves called out a deep primal instinct in a man that left him unable to hold back his hooting and hollering as she roller-bladed by.

Sarah wore string bikinis because they flattered her figure the most. She learned years ago that, as far as swimsuits go, strangely the ones with more material actually made her look fatter. They would cut into her skin the wrong way and cause a bulge here or there. But the string bikinis sat just right and left everything smooth. So, although they were the most revealing, and not something a conservative virgin girl would typically wear, she was stuck with that style because everything else made her look too fat. She also indulged in this one bit of freedom in the one place she was allowed to -- the beach. The rest of her life was so buttoned up and proper, that she allowed herself this small release during her beach time. Her naivety helped too. If she only knew what men were really thinking when they saw her that way, she would never be caught dead in public looking like that. So, for her own good, it was actually helpful that she considered herself overweight, and therefore did not realize how sexy she looked. She was too confident about her life accomplishments to care that she didn't look like a model on the beach. So, believing she was overweight served to allow her the freedom to enjoy the sun in a string bikini.

As Sarah rollerbladed into Venice, White Jr., was purchasing art from a local street vendor. From a distance he saw a woman gliding towards him that could have easily been Sarah. It couldn't be, he thought. Sarah would never reveal that much of herself in public, even on the beach. But as she roller-bladed towards him he could see, it was her! He couldn't believe it! That perfectly put-together prosecutor, so conservative and proper, was out here practically showing all of her tits! Oh, if only he could expose her to their colleagues like this. He could bring her down a notch! He thought about that more and realized, though it might embarrass that perfect little bitch Sarah, nobody else would think it was a big deal because normal people wear swimsuits on the beach, even tiny little swimsuits like the one she had on. No, this would only make her more human, and relatable. It's not what he needed to cut her down. But he was going to watch her, maybe there was more to her than she let on in the courthouse. Maybe she'd get drunk and he could get cell phone video footage of her doing something that would humiliate her before her peers. If he was lucky it would be bad enough to compromise her position with the D.A.'s Office - "conduct unbecoming of an attorney" in their office, something like that. He hid himself from her view and watched as she entered On the Waterfront Cafe.

Cynthia walked in after Sarah had found a table and ordered a beer. The two of them quickly began giggling like schoolgirls. Cynthia was so much fun. She was one of Sarah's best friends. They had a lot in common as far as family values, honesty, and integrity were concerned. But they differed, drastically, on the subject of sex. Sarah was a virgin, waiting for marriage. Cynthia had been a teen-mom whose children were half-grown already. So she didn't need a man for anything but a good time. She was fiercely independent and had worked several jobs to keep her kids in private schools. The thought of marriage sounded like nothing but an extra burden. She also had no interest in developing a serious relationship with a man because she didn't want to expose her children to someone who might not stick around. Never allowing them to completely enter her life, Cynthia used men as play things. She would have a great time with them, enjoy sex with them, then ultimately have to leave them because she couldn't give them a complete relationship. There was a line of men in Cynthia's life who would wait for her call. They were all in love with her and ready to marry her. But Cynthia's life was perfect. She was taking care of her children on her own and she didn't need the complications of a man to ruin what she had.

Today, Cynthia was giving Sarah another lesson in sex-education. Sarah was squeamish about the topic of sex and would sometimes get embarrassed at the stories Cynthia told, but Sarah figured she should probably learn about sex from somewhere so her future husband wouldn't find her boring. So whenever Cynthia would have another great story about the great time she had last night, Sarah considered it a lesson in sex-ed, from a good friend, and she would listen without interruption. Today, Cynthia was talking about "Jiu-Jitsu Guy." Sarah was sure he had a name but she couldn't remember what it was, because Cynthia always called him "Jiu-Jitsu Guy." Cynthia covered her mouth as if about to tell Sarah something unmentionable, and after a lot of giggling, she blurted out, "We broke 2 beds!" Sarah's mouth dropped, she couldn't imagine what in the world people did to break 2 beds! The two of them burst into giggles.

"Oh but I shouldn't tell you this," Cynthia said. "You're little virgin ears probably shouldn't hear it." They laughed again.

Cynthia took a sip of her beer then shook her head at Sarah. "I still can't believe you're really still a virgin. Are you really going to wait until you're married!?"

Sarah nodded. "Yes. I only want to be with one man my whole life. I really believe that if a girl saves herself for marriage, it will make the marriage bond stronger."

Cynthia asked: "What if it's someone who really loves you, will you still make him wait for marriage?"

Sarah answered: "I'll know he loves me, when he marries me."

Sarah was dead certain about this one thing. She would never compromise on this one thing. She would never compromise her virtue for what might end up being a short-lived romance. She believed that marriage was supposed to be for life and she believed that a person would live a much higher quality of life and a much happier marriage if they committed themselves to that one and only partner. She looked forward to her wedding night with her dream man, whoever that might be. She wanted to experience that special moment of giving herself to him on the day they got married. Her virginity was important to her. She thought it should be treasured and held protected for the one and only man who would be her husband, the one who was meant to love her and cherish her forever. The one she would have children with and grow old with. This was one of the most important things in Sarah's life, and she wanted to treasure it and share it with her husband one day.

As Sarah explained all this to Cynthia while they sat at the table sipping their beers, she was completely unaware that White Jr., was sitting behind her listening to it all. He had stealthily snuck in and found a seat behind Sarah where he could watch and listen to everything she was doing. He was in shock to hear what he had just heard. Sarah was a virgin. When he heard her say that, his eyes widened and his mouth dropped. And he stared at her. He listened intently as she described how important her virginity was to her and he just stared, looking her up and down, from head to toe, taking in every inch of her body with his eyes, sinister thoughts running through his head. He knew exactly what he was going to do to her now. He knew exactly how to destroy this perfect little bitch.

CHAPTER 8

On Tuesday evening, David was at a charity event where the city was honoring its fallen heroes. David had a lot of money and he believed it was his duty to give back to the community. He donated to many charities. This one tugged at his heartstrings the most. It was meant to help the spouses and children of police officers who had fallen in the line of duty. David lost his own father as a young child and he wanted to help children who lost their parents, particularly when their parents had sacrificed their lives to keep others safe. David was also a large contributor to charities meant for military families. This evening's event was a dinner. The price of each plate included a donation to the charity. Donors were also encouraged to write checks, if they wished to contribute more. David wrote a very large check. He did every year. But David didn't like to receive recognition for his charitable donations. He gave out of the kindness of his heart, not out of a desire to be recognized. So he left the party early, after each hero had been recognized, but before they began thanking the donors. It was still early, so David went to his favorite bar for a drink.

Sarah sat at the bar in The Blvd at the Beverly Wilshire Hotel. She took a sip of her apple martini. It was a little tart, a little sweet and a lot strong. The perfect drink to help her forget about her stressful day at the D.A.'s Office. A few sips into her perfectly poured beverage, a warm happiness entered Sarah's heart. It was the feeling a person gets when first seeing a loved one who has been gone for far too long. Though she didn't know it, it was the presence of the man who stood behind her that caused this feeling to arise in her heart. Then, she heard his voice. As he spoke over her shoulder to give the bar tender his drink order, Sarah indulged in the sweet sound of his smooth, buttery and very masculine voice.

The new feelings the sound of his voice invoked in her made Sarah think of Mick Jagger. She remembered a comedian using Mick Jagger as an example when he joked about how the most unattractive men with the best voices always get laid. She then wondered if that voice she heard belonged to a good-looking man or an unattractive man. Feeling playful, she spun around 180 degrees on her barstool. What she saw took her breath away. She gazed up into David's deep blue eyes and stared into them -- speechless.

Sarah felt a calm she's never felt before. Instantly, her whole body felt relaxed. A small delicate sigh escaped her lips, and she began to feel an aching desire between her legs. Although Sarah was a virgin, she was familiar with sexual desire and pleasure. She knew the feel of a man's hands between her legs. Valuing her virginity too much, she had never allowed a prior boyfriend to slip his finger inside, but she had known the feel of a man's hands fondling her clitoris until she orgasamed. In this moment, she yearned for David's touch in that way. She also yearned for something more, something she didn't quite understand because she had never felt it before. She felt an aching deeper inside her now, a place no one had ever been. She wanted to be as close to David as she could possibly be. The few inches between them felt like a great distance that was far too wide. Without being consciously aware of it, Sarah's body involuntarily moved closer towards David, her eyes falling to his lips now as if they were about to kiss.

Just then, her phone rang. The shrill of the "old phone" ringtone set for work-related calls ripped Sarah from the dreamy moment and brought her mind back to reality. She jerked backwards to a more respectable distance and answered the call. She jumped off her barstool and nervously uttered "excuse me," as she hurried past David outside so that she could speak to the caller in private. She did not want this magnificent blue-eyed stranger to hear her cuss like a sailor if she had to, as she frequently did during these typical mid-night calls from police officers at crime scenes calling to check in with her about criminal procedure, preservation of evidence, and insuring they were not about to cross the line of constitutionality and render the evidence they've gathered inadmissible in a court of law. She quickly found the exit without looking back at David.

DAMN IT! DAMN IT! HOW COULD HE LET HER SLIP AWAY AGAIN!? David thought. He stood there angry with himself. She was right there, right in front of him. All he had to do was speak. At least five minutes had passed before her phone rang. That was plenty of time for him to work his magic. David never let a girl get away once he had her attention. He always knew what to say. But today, his smooth-talking mouth betrayed him. He just stood there, stupidly staring at her. It wasn't like him. David knew how to speak to women. He knew what they all wanted to hear. He could quickly figure out what a particular woman was interested in, with just a few initial questions at the beginning of a conversation. He could capture her attention and engage her in dazzling conversation for as long as it took to lure her into his bed. But today, David had no clue what to say to this dark-haired beauty. He didn't want to lure her to his bed. He wanted to love and cherish her. He wanted to get to know her.

He wanted her to know him. He wanted to build a strong foundation--something they could rest true love on, forever. He wanted the kind of comfort and ease he observed between his parents when he was a child. He remembered his father describing how long it took him to win-over his mother before their first kiss. He had always said: "Son, everlasting love requires a strong foundation. You have to build that first before you ask a woman to be your wife. One day, when you're a man, you're going to find a woman as good as your mother. Make sure you don't scare her away by moving too quickly. Remember to build the foundation first, before you ask for her hand, or even before you try for that first kiss." David was young enough back then to think kissing was gross. He always said "Eew!" when his father would finish that sentence. And his father would chuckle. But his father's words came to him now and they meant everything.

David realized then, that his suaveness was always used in the wrong way. He used it on women who wanted his money. He used it on women who hoped to land a leading role in one of his movies. He used it on women who just liked a good time and who kept loose morals so that high standards wouldn't interfere with their fun. But he had no idea what to do if he wanted to build a foundation for everlasting love. Feeling that ineptitude, David decided it was best to re-group before he saw that dark-haired beauty again. So he motioned for Louis, his favorite bartender, who came right over. David slipped Louis a $100 bill.

"How can I help you, David?"

"The girl who was sitting here, get me her name, first and last. Find out as much as you can about her in that friendly bartender way."

"Oh, you like Sarah."

"Sarah? That's her name? What's her last name?"

"Dunno, she normally pays with cash," Louis said.

"Well, don't let her this time. Tell her you don't have change or something"

"Ha, Ha, Ha! At the Beverly Wilshire Hotel?"

"Well, think of something!"

"Don't worry, David. I will let you know everything you need to know."

And with that, David left the bar. He trusted Louis. But more than that, he had a strong feeling he would see her again, even without Louis' help. David felt this inexplicable certainty that they would meet again. That calmed him and helped him focus on his game plan -- learning how to build that foundation. What was his opening line going to be when he finally spoke to his future wife? He hated thinking of his first words to her as a pickup line. But then what else was a man's opening line to a woman he was interested in, but a pick up line? That is what had caused David's loss of words. How could he speak to her like she was one of his many conquests? That was the last thing he wanted to do. He needed a lot of time to think about this. David tipped the valet driver and slipped into the driver's seat of his new car. On his drive home to his Malibu mansion, David coasted up Pacific Coast Highway and thought about Sarah. He realized that fear was part of what paralyzed him when he stood there face to face with her. For as much as his heart wanted her, he also felt an equal amount of fear that she would reject him.

When Sarah ended the call and re-entered The Blvd, she looked around for David but did not see him. Feeling a stab of disappointment, she left enough money next to her drink to cover the bill and a tip. She then slipped away while Louis was helping another customer at the other end of the bar. Louis looked up as he saw Sarah's long dark hair disappear around the corner. He called her name but she didn't hear him.

CHAPTER 9

White Jr., waited three weeks for this. It had been about that long since he'd heard Sarah say she was a virgin. He spent about a week trying to come up with his plan. He spent two weeks trying to lure Sarah to a place private enough for him to execute his plan. It wasn't easy. He couldn't think of a way to get her somewhere private that was not work-related. So he decided the conference room of his father's law firm would have to do. It had no exterior windows. Though there was an entire wall of glass, it was a window that faced only the interior of the office suite. And it was fitting. He wanted to do this to her in a place she associated with her work.

Sarah worked most nights, weekends, and holidays, so it would be easy. Labor Day was coming up and all his staff would have the day off. His father and his father's partner would be gone too because they would be traveling for the three-day weekend. Although another law firm occupied the same floor of the office building in which White, White & Smith had their offices, the office suites were separate. So, even if that law firm was open on Labor Day, he would have enough space and privacy in the office suite occupied by White, White & Smith to execute on his plan.

White Jr., had called Sarah and told her that he represented a witness who had video evidence that exonerated a defendant charged with armed robbery in one of Sarah's cases. If she wanted to view the video, she had to meet him in his office on Labor Day. The trial was scheduled to begin about a week after that, and Sarah had an ethical duty and a responsibility under the constitution to bring forth evidence that tended to prove the defendant was innocent. She was required to watch the video and present it to the defense. Therefore, she could not decline White Jr.'s suggested meeting. He told her that out of his firm's respect for her, he wanted her to see it first so that she would not be blind-sided with it during trial. She bought his story, hook, line and sinker. He left the door to the office suite unlocked so that she could let herself in. She knew their offices well, so he told her to let herself in and meet him in the conference room where he would have the video set up.

On Labor Day, White Jr., waited anxiously in the conference room. When he heard Sarah open the door to the office suite, he stood up. He had to move quickly while he still had the element of surprise in his favor. He could see Sarah walking towards the conference room and he thought to himself, "Lucky me, she's in a dress today." As soon as Sarah walked into the conference room, White Jr., knocked her down. She was on the floor now, still shocked by what had happened. He threw himself on top of her. It was in that moment that Sarah realized what was happening.

Sarah began fighting, kicking and screaming. She was scratching and swinging at him, trying anything she could to get him off of her. White Jr., grabbed her hands to stop her, but he needed one hand free so he could reach up and yank off her underwear. With all her squirming and kicking it was hard to get her underwear off with only one hand. She was cussing and kicking and spitting in his face. She even tried to bite him. "Ooooh, yeah, bite me," he taunted, "I like it rough too, you little whore." Disgusted, Sarah fought harder. She was able to free the hand he had pinned down. Now, she had both her hands free and she began clawing at his eyeballs. She was going to rip them out of his face. But he was too fast. This time he grabbed both her hands and held her down for a long time, rubbing his erection against her clothes. "I'm going to warm you up first," he said. "Feel that," he demanded, "This is what cock feels like. I know you've never felt one of these inside you before. I'm going to give you your first introduction, so that you can never, ever have sex with anyone else, without thinking of me. Ha, ha, ha," he laughed menacingly, "You little bitch. You've always thought you were better than me. Well who's got the better of who, now?"

Struggling as much as she could to free her hands and wiggle her body out from under him, Sarah was getting tired. White Jr., could feel her getting tired. The struggle was slowing, so, he was going to hold her down for longer. He would make sure she was out of strength before he tried pulling her underwear off again. Her dress crept up high enough during the struggle, that all he needed to do now was pull her underwear out of the way. He teased her. He loosened his grip just barely to make her believe she had a chance of freeing herself. It worked. She began fighting harder, but she couldn't get her hands free. He was going to make her work harder at this for a good long while. She was stronger and feistier than he ever imagined. Oh he knew, she'd fight him, but her strength surprised him. So he toyed with her. He just needed to keep her hands secure long enough to make her lose her strength. He could still feel a good struggle, so he kept both her hands pinned. He made sure to keep his groin away from her knees. She was trying to bring her legs up to kick him with her knee. But he could read her strategy, now. He would just let her keep trying, teasing her a little with the opportunity to kick him there, he would move his groin within range then thrust up real quick, slamming himself against her vagina over her underwear.

This sick dance went on for a while. Finally, he felt her struggle seemed a little weaker. So, in one foul swooped, as quick as he could, he released one hand and yanked her underwear half way down her thighs. This was far enough to do the job, but he wanted them all the way off. If he could've, he would've gotten her entirely naked before forcing himself inside her. But she'd get away if he tried that, so he couldn't risk it. So he kept yanking and yanking until the underwear was around her ankles. He decided to leave them there, as sort of a rope keeping her from being able to kick with her feet. Feeling exposed, Sarah quickly cupped her free hand over her vagina, creating a protective barrier. She would hold it there, like a chastity belt and was not going to let him in. Satisfied that he had restrained her enough, White, Jr., thrust his erection towards her vagina. He thrust and thrust but he could not enter. So he thrust again, and again, harder and harder, but still, he couldn't penetrate. What the? Then, he looked down and realized her hand was there, he grabbed that hand and yanked it above her head.

With her underwear out of the way, he could now use both of his hands to restrain her hands above her head. Pinning both her hands down as hard as he could, not allowing the slightest bit of room for her to even wiggle her wrists, pressing his arms down onto hers to further pin her in an immobile position, he used his knee to force her legs apart. There, he thought. Now he's got her in the right position. She can't move out of his grasp now. He's going to take his sweet time, so he could feel every inch of himself slowly entering her. He'll save the hard thrusting for when he's all the way inside her, after he penetrates deep enough that she can't wiggle him out. He began at her inner thigh just above the knee, pressing his hard cock against her skin, slowly sliding it up towards her vagina. He wanted to feel every inch of her skin on his way up, prolonging the moment of his pleasure. He wanted her to feel every inch of him sliding up towards her virginity, prolonging the torment he wanted to inflict on her. Feeling defenseless, knowing she can't get out of this position, and fearing he was about to rape her precious virginity out of her, Sarah screamed a blood curling scream so loud, it seemed to shake the windows. The scream even startled White Jr., frozen. "Shut up, bitch!" he screamed at her, "Most women beg for this. Shut the fuck up!"

After regaining his composure, White Jr., started over again, pressing his hard cock against the inside of her leg, next to her knee, he continued his upward movement. Just before the tip of his penis reached the entrance of her vagina, like magic, White Jr., suddenly floated off of her. She watched as White Jr.'s body flung through the air, crashing against the window of the conference room, glass shattering all around him. As she watched him crash through the glass, Sarah shoved her dress down to cover herself and began scrambling to her feet. Then, she saw what had flung White, Jr., through the air. It was him. It was that blue-eyed man whose face had captured her heart and soul three weeks ago. He stood above her now, reaching out his hand to help her up. David looked into Sarah's eyes, and in a very serious, almost frightening voice, he demanded: "Get out." She blinked at him, confused. What did he say? As he turned towards White, Jr., David looked over his shoulder at Sarah, and said: "I don't want you to see this." She then realized, the blue-eyed man was about to do what she wanted to do. He was going to kill White, Jr.

David slowly and deliberately walked towards White Jr., his rage greater than he could control. He didn't know how he was going to kill him, but he knew one thing was certain -- he was not going to allow that man to walk out of there alive. David thought of slicing his throat with the broken glass that lay all around him on the floor. He thought of hitting him, kicking him, slamming his head into the ground and beating him until near death to ensure he felt as much pain as possible, before David choked the life out of him. Yes. That is what he would do. David was going to kill White, Jr., with his bare hands.

When David first charged into that room at the sound of a woman in peril, which he heard stepping off the elevator on his way to meet his entertainment lawyer, David had not known who the woman was. He just rushed in as fast as he could to help, whoever it was. That blood-curling scream gripping him from deep inside, propelling him to move quickly before it was too late, David barged in and immediately saw the threat. He picked the man up and threw him off her. Then, he saw her. It was that brunette who stirred his soul so deeply that he knew, upon first sight of her, that she would be his wife. Now that he had seen who that scumbag piece of shit had assaulted, David could only feel pure rage strong enough to make him want to commit murder. Sarah watched as David walked deliberately towards White, Jr., who was trying to pick himself up, bloody and moaning in pain from the broken glass that was lodged into his skin, all over his body. But Sarah couldn't let David do it. Her mind flashed to an image of David's murder trial. She felt soul-wrenching fear that the jury would convict. She pictured David in the defendant's seat while the foreman of the jury stood to deliver the verdict. Sarah screamed: "No! Noooooo! Don't do it!" David stopped. Until then, he hadn't realized she was still in the room. He couldn't kill a man right in front of her, but he was still so angry. He couldn't let this coward, this scum, survive. He had to pay for what he'd done. Sarah knew she had slowed down the blue-eyed man, but she wasn't sure she had stopped him. So she ran to him and grabbed one shoulder, looking into his deep blue eyes, she begged: "Please. Please. YOU take me away from here. Take me somewhere safe." David's heart melted as he saw those beautiful brown eyes, pleading with him. How could he have forgotten to take care of her? He was so focused on destroying the thing that had threatened her, he'd forgotten that she would need his care, that she would need him more than ever in these first moments after the attack. So he grabbed her hand and said, "Let's go." They ran out of there together, holding hands. They left White, Jr., a bloody mess on the floor.

CHAPTER 10

As they entered the garage of the office building that David and Sarah were fleeing, David led Sarah with a firm, comforting grip of her hand, in a fast-paced walk towards a yellow Lamborghini. The irony of it was not lost on Sarah. Her hero was not whisking her away on a big white horse like in a romance novel, but this was pretty much a modern day version of that scene. That car. This man, with those blue eyes she'd dreamt of every night since she first stared into them the night she lost him at The Blvd., was now rescuing her away from White, White & Smith in the one car they never thought to use as bait to entice her away from the D.A.'s Office. It was a bright, shiny, brand new yellow Lamborghini - her dream car, ever since she was a child. The vision of it made everything feel even more surreal. Was she in a nightmare? Was she in a dream? Everything happened so fast, Sarah was in a mental haze. She just followed David silently, as he led her to his car, opened the door for her, sat her down and buckled her seat belt. She felt safe with him. He had rescued her. His presence calmed her. There was such a familiar comfort Sarah felt with David, that she actually forgot he was a complete stranger.

David pulled out of the garage in a hurry. He wanted to get Sarah out of that horrible place as fast as he could. She had just been assaulted there, so he needed to get her out of there quickly. "Take me somewhere safe," she had said to him. Her words rang in his ears. It was his duty to protect her. It was his mission to get her somewhere safe as fast as he could. There was only one place he could think of. He wanted to take her there and protect her for the rest of her life. There was no safer place she could be. He was taking her to his sanctuary. His beautiful mansion in Malibu had a magnificent ocean view and grounds so expansive that a person could retreat there for months without ever getting bored. He would tell her she could stay as long as she needed to.

David whipped through the streets of downtown LA until he reached the 101. He sped past all the cars, weaving in and out of them, until he exited onto the 405, which was always gridlocked. He cussed under his breath but Sarah didn't hear it over the roar of his engine. When they finally reached the 10, David sped up again. Sarah felt so safe with David that she forgot to even ask him where he was taking her. Strangely, this was her way home. But on the 10 they past the exit Sarah would normally get off, and her hazy illogical thought that this man knew where she lived, faded away.

David and Sarah had sat in his car in silence during the entire drive. Sarah was in too much of a mental haze to think or speak. David was worried about her psychological and emotional state and decided it was best to leave her in silence until she felt like speaking. As the 10 turned into Pacific Coast Highway, the ocean came into view and Sarah and David each breathed a sigh of relief. Now, they finally felt far enough away from that horrible scene that they could each breathe a little easier. David cruised up Pacific Coast Highway towards Malibu and Sarah sat patiently and silently in his car.

As they approached the grand iron gates of his sanctuary, David stopped his car and swiped his card to open the gates. He then looked at

Sarah while they waited for the gates to open, and he asked her softly: "Is this ok?" She looked into his eyes and nodded, "Yes."

He was happy he had her permission to take her past the gates. He knew she would be in a delicate state of mind and he didn't want to scare her. They drove up his long drive way to his home and they walked in through the front door. They were alone. David did not have staff at his Malibu mansion because this was the place he liked to retreat to alone. He would call in a cleaning crew only on an as-needed basis, but he did all his own cooking here. He made his own coffee, and enjoyed the privacy and solitude of his sanctuary. He knew Sarah would want privacy after the attack, so this was a good place for her now.

As soon as they walked in, Sarah's knees gave way. Suddenly, she was so weak from the stress of her ordeal that she couldn't stand. David caught her before she fell. He was holding her in his arms now, the way a groom would carry his bride over the threshold.

Embarrassed, Sarah apologized. "I'm sorry, I just suddenly felt so weak."

"It's ok. Don't apologize, I got you."

"I think, I need to lay down for a while."

"Yes. Of course."

David carried Sarah up the stairs to his bedroom. He laid her down on his big, soft luxurious bed covered in white satin sheets and a pure white down comforter. His thick, elegant white drapes were open and the view of the ocean from his bed put Sarah at ease. One window was open, letting in the fresh ocean breeze, adding an even more relaxed atmosphere to the elegance of this heavenly place. Sarah lay on her back and exhaled a long exasperated sigh as she sank deeper into that soft bed. David didn't know what to do. He thought she would need her privacy but she looked so vulnerable he didn't want to leave her alone. So he sat on the bed and just watched her, waiting for a hint of what she preferred.

Sarah lay on the bed with her eyes closed for a moment, the strain of the day still showing in her face. David wanted to touch her face gently. He wanted to stroke her hair. He wanted to comfort her. She looked so delicate, so frail, so vulnerable, he just wanted to hold her in his arms and tell her that everything would be ok. But he couldn't touch her. He didn't want to frighten her. Then, with her eyes still closed, Sarah reached for David's hand. He grabbed on tight with both of his hands. "I'm here. I'm still here. I won't leave you. Tell me what you want me to do." Sarah whispered with a vulnerable plea, "will you please hold me?" David's arms had felt so strong and so safe as he carried her up the stairs, she needed to feel that security again. She felt exposed and vulnerable lying on the bed alone. She yearned for the safety she felt in his arms. He was her hero, and she needed to feel his protection.

David immediately responded to her request. He slid in close to her and gently wrapped his strong arms around her. "I'm here. You're safe." Sarah nuzzled her face into David's chest and she began to cry.

David held her strong in his arms and let her cry. He knew she needed to release all the negativity she had experienced, so he didn't try to shush her. He wanted her to get it all out. Between sobs, Sarah said, "You saved me! You saved me! Thank you so much! Thank you so much for saving me!" As her hard, sobbing cry whaled on, David just held her and listened. She went on. "He... he... he almost..."

Almost? The word "almost" made David sigh with relief. He understood the significance of that one word. It meant the rapist had not achieved his goal. When David barged into that office after hearing her blood-curling scream, he only saw White Jr., on top of her. It appeared that the rape was already underway. To hear Sarah say "he almost" gave David so much relief. He had reached her in time! Maybe she could recover from this experience completely. He had reached her in time! He was so happy it was only "almost" a rape. He hoped and prayed that this meant Sarah would not be haunted by this for the rest of her life, that she would recover and be a complete person again.

Her next words stopped David's heart. "I'm still a virgin because of you. Thank you, my hero."

A virgin!?!?! Oh my God, David thought. A flood of emotions rushed through him. He was confused. He was shocked. He was nervous. He was full of rage at how that scumbag almost took her virginity in that way. Thoughts of murdering him rushed back into his head. Then he remembered; the rapist was unsuccessful. Sarah was still intact. She was still innocent and pure. She was now safe in his arms and he would never, ever let anyone come near her again. David squeezed his arms around her tighter. He rocked her like a child in his arms. "Shssshhh," he whispered, "Shhsshhh. Everything is going to be ok." He spoke to calm himself more so than to calm her. He rocked her gently in his arms waiting for his racing heart to slow down. He couldn't believe this beautiful woman who had stolen his heart, the one he knew upon first sight of her to be his future wife, was still a virgin. He couldn't believe how close he'd come to losing that precious gift before they ever had a chance to love each other. In his heart, he was thanking God profusely for letting him get there in time to save her.

David held Sarah in his arms until all her crying was out of her system. She then nuzzled against his chest and fell asleep. He watched her for a while before falling asleep himself.

A few hours later, as night fell, a cold breeze burst into David's room, waking him with a chill. He stirred a little and slowly began to release his hold of Sarah. This woke Sarah.

"Where are you going!?" she cried desperately.

"Nowhere. I'm still here. I'm just going to close the window."

"I don't want to be alone."

"I know," he whispered gently, "It'll just be a second. I'm just closing the window."

As David walked over to the window, Sarah felt gripping fear at the void he left her with. She hated being without the comfort of his arms around her. She was still shaken-up and afraid. She only felt safe in David's arms. He had just barely reached the window, when she said: "Come back!"

David hurried with the window and rushed back to the bed. He could hear the desperation and vulnerability in her voice. He knew she was still afraid and still needed the comfort of his arms. So he rushed back to bed and held her close, "I'm never going to leave you. I will hold you as long as you need me to." Sarah began to cry again, silently this time, tears streaming down her face. She had always been a strong and independent woman. She believed nothing could bring her down. But this, this experience left her terrified. She was weak. She was desperate. She needed a good man to protect her. She needed the warmth and safety she felt from David to wash away the terror and disgust she felt when White Jr., assaulted her. Only David's presence could wash away those thoughts and terrible feelings. She wondered how long she was going to feel this way, so needy and vulnerable. She wondered if she was going to feel like a scared, desperate little girl her whole life.

David did everything he could to comfort and soothe Sarah. He wanted to put positive thoughts in her mind before she fell asleep again. So he began describing the beautiful grounds surrounding his home.

"Sarah, tomorrow is a new day. In the morning light, I'm going to show you the most beautiful things. I have a waterfall and a stream in my back yard. I have every kind of fruit tree you can imagine. I have nut trees too. The grass is soft and green and lush. It looks like the Garden of Eden out there. And I can't wait to show it to you."

David went on, "I have horses. Do you like horses?"

"Yes." Sarah smiled as she wiped away her tears.

"I have this beautiful little colt that you're going to love. You know, horses all have their own personalities. This one is sweet. He loves people. When I go to feed him, he isn't interested in the food. He just wants to be petted and loved. He's going to love you. I call him 'Sam.' Do you want to meet Sam tomorrow morning?"

"Yes," she whispered.

"Then, I'll introduce you to Sam."

David continued describing his beautiful grounds to Sarah and describing all the fun things they would do tomorrow, until Sarah fell asleep to the sweet sound of his voice. When he was certain that she had fallen into a deep enough slumber that she would be asleep the whole night, he relaxed and fell asleep too.

CHAPTER 11

Bright sunlight streamed into David's bedroom. The birds were chirping loudly and cheerfully outside. Sarah woke up with a smile. She felt a lightness in her heart. All the negativity she felt from yesterday's ordeal had been released through all the crying she let out last night. It helped that David was by her side keeping her safe the whole time. This gave her strength.

David was right. Today was a new day. Sarah felt cheerful. She felt happy. She felt hopeful for the future. Most importantly, she felt safe. David was still by her side. She looked at him now. He looked so sweet and innocent while he slept. She smiled at him and lay back down, nuzzling next to him, listening to the heavy breathing sound of his sleep. He sounded sweet, she thought. She liked the rhythm of his breath. It was loud enough to almost be a snore but not quite. She thought that was cute. But she was ready for him to be awake now, so she gently nudged him, hoping he'd wake up. David stirred, but remained sleeping. Sarah sighed and waited. She decided she should let him sleep because he was so wonderful to her last night, holding her while she cried, helping her through the night. His beautiful words had filled her head with positive thoughts. She dreamt of being in a park with him, picking fruit and laughing in the sun.

Suddenly, a crazy thought popped into Sarah's mind. *"Oh no! I don't know his name!"* Sarah was shocked by the sudden realization of that fact. Things had happened so quickly yesterday, the stress of the day's events, the high emotions, and his sweet nurturing care -- it all had them so caught up in dealing with the drama, that they had forgotten to introduce themselves to each other. Sarah searched for rational thought. How could this be? She felt so safe with this man. It felt like they'd known each other their whole lives. She felt nurtured and protected by him, as if he were a man who had loved her for a long time. That is why she had forgotten to ask him his name. Then she remembered; this magnificent blue-eyed stranger called her Sarah last night. How did he know her name, but she did not know his? Sarah wondered if they'd had that conversation in the car. Possibly she answered him absent-mindedly and simply forgot now. But she had no memory of any conversation in the car.

The fact was, David remembered Sarah's name from when Louis had told him that night at The Blvd. But Sarah had no way of knowing that. Lying next to David, feeling guilty that she couldn't remember his name, Sarah justified the situation to herself with the explanation that she had been through a lot yesterday, so he would just have to forgive her for needing to ask his name today.

Finally, David woke up. He smiled brightly at Sarah. "Good morning," he said.

"Good morning," she smiled shyly at him. Then Sarah said, "I have a question for you."

"What is it?"

Sarah hesitated, shy to ask him.

"What?" he asked her. "You can ask me anything."

"Ummm..." She tilted her head to the side and looked up at him, sheepishly. She then quickly and shyly blurted out: "What's your name?"

David burst into laughter. She was so cute! She was shy to ask his name. Of course, they had forgotten to introduce themselves yesterday with all that went on! After a long hardy laugh, and with a warm, bright smile, David looked at Sarah and cheerfully said: "I'm David!"

Sarah smiled sweetly at him, her soft brown eyes, gleaming, "It's nice to meet you David." The two of them giggled together, their faces inches apart. David lost himself in the romance of it, and he leaned in and kissed Sarah softly on the lips. She returned his kiss with pleasure and the two of them engaged in a long, passionate, French kiss that they both needed so desperately.

When David finally lifted his mouth off Sarah's and smiled down at her. Sarah said, "Wow, it's really nice to meet you, David."

David smiled and looked down at her warmly, but he did not want things to get steamy. He wanted to respect Sarah. So he sat up and said, "Do you want breakfast? I can make you pancakes!"

Sarah squealed, excitedly, "I love pancakes!"

The two of them giggled like children then hurried downstairs together towards the kitchen.

In the kitchen, David stirred the pancake batter and Sarah squeezed the oranges for the fresh squeezed orange juice. The two of them worked in the kitchen together with the ease and comfort of a couple who had been together for years. And it felt like they were a couple. Sarah had to keep reminding herself that she just met this man. But then she'd force the thought out of her mind with reckless abandon, thinking, *"I'm just going to enjoy this! Why shouldn't I enjoy this!?"*

As they finished breakfast, Sarah asked David to do her a small favor. Obviously, she needed time off work, but she couldn't bear the thought of making the phone call and answering a bunch of questions about why she wasn't coming in for a while. So, she asked David if he would do that for her.

"Absolutely!" David said. He gave her his phone and said, "Just dial. I'll do all the talking."

David spoke to the appropriate person who needed to be notified of Sarah's absence. He made up a detailed story about how Sarah had fallen ill and it was doctor's orders that she take at least three weeks off from work. Sarah had only told David to tell them she would be out a few days, but David thought she would need much more time than that, so he took charge and demanded that her work relent to her personal needs.

Sarah was grateful as she heard him on the phone. Deep down she wanted a lot of time off but she had been such a determined workaholic for so many years, she just didn't know how to ask for desperately needed personal time.

David felt a little guilty about the secret hope he held inside that the extended request for leave would cause her to lose her job and require her to depend on him. He knew without a doubt that this woman was going to be his wife. He wouldn't have it any other way, so why should she be burdened with a job? No wife of his would have to work. Of course, he wouldn't dare voice these thoughts out loud. Giving up her job to marry him was a choice Sarah had to make on her own. And David was going to be as patient as he needed to be, waiting for that to happen.

Before taking Sarah outside to show her the day he had promised her, David thought they should discuss one very important matter. He didn't want to bring it up, but since they had just taken care of the work call, he thought this was the appropriate time. He looked at her now with all seriousness, and spoke carefully and gently.

"Sarah, do you want me to call the police to come over here and take a statement from you so that we don't have to go to the police station?"

Sarah's eyes widened, as fear came back to her face, "No!" she demanded. "No! I can't talk to the police about this!"

"Sarah, Sarah, it's ok. I'll do whatever you want to do. It's your choice," David wrapped his arms around her as he spoke those words, wanting to comfort her again. He didn't want her to slip backwards into the memory of what had happened to her. He held her as she grabbed onto him tightly.

She spoke into his shoulder, "I can't David. I work with the police. I instruct them in their investigations. I can't have them viewing me as a victim. I can't have them picturing me in that scene with White Jr., a low life who has no respect from anyone in the courthouse, doing *that* to *me*."

"It's ok, Sarah. I understand. It's up to you. It's completely up to you."

She looked up into David's eyes now. "David, can we just pretend like it never happened? He didn't get what he wanted. In the end, we won. You threw him through that glass, and he was all bloody. He will take a long time to recover from that. That's justice enough for me, especially because he didn't really accomplish anything. He just wrestled me to the ground, that's all. That's how I want to view it now. It'll be easier for me to just view it that way and forget the whole thing. I can't let people look at me as if I'm a weak woman who was victimized by a man."

David understood. He remembered how powerful she looked standing in front of that table full of old, gray-haired lawyers who were looking up at her, hanging on her every word as she spoke of her courtroom battles. He remembered how visible their respect for her was. He understood that Sarah's career, her reputation, depended on her image of strength. He understood that she could not allow her peers and colleagues to view her in a sexual light, especially not in a position of weakness. David nodded as he looked into Sarah's face. "Yes, Sarah. I think you are absolutely right. Nothing happened. It was just a wrestling match, that he lost."

David decided that he would stick to Sarah's description of what had occurred. He knew that this was how she chose to deal with it and move on. He didn't think there was any harm in letting her deny the magnitude of the incident because, thankfully, she was not actually raped. She still had her virtue intact and that would give her strength. That would allow her to brush off the incident and truly lead her life as if nothing had happened. Also, David wanted his cheerful Sarah back. The one who innocently giggled in bed with him, the one he had fun making breakfast with. And if all he had to do was agree with her censored version of the story, he would do that.

David kissed Sarah gently and kindly asked her to join him in the Garden of Eden.

Sarah and David walked into his backyard, which, was very large but didn't seem as gigantic as she had pictured when he described his grounds last night. She saw the horse stables over to the right and wanted to meet Sam, but David was walking her straight ahead instead, towards a solid wall of tall fir trees. It felt as if they were entering a forest behind his house. But as they neared, Sarah could see that it wasn't a forest. Instead, it was a boundary made 1-tree deep of a long row of fir trees, serving as a hidden fence. Behind the line of fir trees was an actual iron gate that surrounded the most beautiful thing Sarah had ever seen. It was a large clearing of lush green grass and rolling hills, bright flowers of all different kinds and all different colors all around. Fruit trees scattered all around providing shade and juicy fruit that you could pick right off the tree and eat where you were standing. Sarah could hear running water that sounded much too powerful to be coming from the stream that she could see as David unlocked the gate and invited her in.

"I'm the only one with key," he said. "Nobody gets in here without me letting them in. This gate and this row of fir trees surrounds the entire

30-acre area, giving the utmost privacy and serenity that you could hope to find anywhere in the world. The only things this gate can't keep out are God's creatures who are meant to live in this environment. Deer jump the fence and roam at leisure in here. They're used to me. They come right up to me sometimes. They'll just stand two feet away from me and look at me, as they eat my flowers, as if I planted them here for the deer to eat. But I've never been able to pet one. If I reach my hand towards them, they'll dart away from me, quick as lightening. So I have to just enjoy being able to watch them. I guess they're not meant to be touched; only seen.

I also see the most beautiful colored birds and butterflies fluttering around here. It's like they all know this place is meant for them to flourish. Usually, I just sit here and enjoy it all happening all around me. This is where I come to think. This is where I come to relax. This is my first place of retreat when I'm down, or stressed, or angry. This place always makes everything all right. And I hope it gives you the same feeling too."

Sarah was amazed. She couldn't believe her eyes. She was speechless. David could see in her face how much she loved this place. When she finally caught her breath, she looked at him and said: "It's amazing."

Then Sarah asked, "Where's the sound of that water coming from?"

"Come here, I'll show you."

David grabbed Sarah's hand and walked her past a large hill. As they rounded the corner, Sarah saw it. It was an enormous waterfall, falling powerfully into the stream, surrounded by full trees, bright flowers and chirping birds. This was David's Garden of Eden.

David and Sarah spent the majority of the day in the Garden of Eden. They sat on the bank of the stream near the waterfall and put their feet in the water. "This is soooo incredible," Sarah said. "It feels like paradise!"

"It's my paradise," David said. "And now you can share it with me."

Sarah leaned towards David with a giggle and he kissed her chastely on the lips. They sat there for a long time as David described what they were looking at. His giant waterfall looked natural, but it was actually man-made. He had it installed because he had an image in his mind of what the perfect picture of nature's beauty included. God made the ocean he could see out the front of his house, but his large property in the back needed more beauty, and there was so much room for David to play with. So he created this paradise. He had all the fruit and nut trees planted. He made sure the greenest grass was maintained. He had colorful flowers planted all around and demanded that most of them be of the type that never died, but lived year round. For variety, he let them plant flowers that were seasonal, but he required a splash of color to keep his beautiful place lively all year round.

He had the waterfall installed in such a way that made it look natural. In fact, it was just a giant fountain embedded into the natural rock to appear as if the water flowed naturally from the rock. It pooled into a stream that was made with the same technology you see in lazy-river pools at some resorts. He made it so that the stream would wind down the hill and around the rock, so that from here, it looked like it went on forever. But in fact, the water was funneled right back into the rock to fall back down the waterfall. It was essentially, recycled water so that there would be no waste. The water went through a filtration system in the rock so that the water was always clean. He wanted to be able to take a dip in it, anytime he wanted to. As David described this all to Sarah, she looked up at the waterfall in awe. And David secretly yearned for the day that he and Sarah would skinny dip in his stream, next to the waterfall.

David and Sarah walked around his property, eating fruit and nuts right off the trees. They strolled over to the horses where Sarah got to meet Sam. He was every bit as lovable and sweet as David had described. She petted him to her heart's content. When she walked away from him, he made a loud neigh sound, as if calling her to come back and pet him some more. She laughed and couldn't resist his cute, baby horse's call. She ran back and pet him some more. David watched her adoringly. He loved the way her beautiful face lit up as she interacted with the animals.

As day turned to night, David and Sarah headed back to the house. David's assistant was calling from the front gate of his house to be let in. She was there to bring the new wardrobe David had instructed her to purchase for Sarah so that Sarah wouldn't have to leave his sanctuary for the whole three weeks she would take off work. This caught Sarah by surprise. David had made the call to his assistant when Sarah was in the bathroom, changing into clothing she borrowed from his closet. His shorts were too big for her, but they had fastened them with a belt. She swam in his extra large t-shirt, except for the part that landed on her large breasts. He loved seeing her wear his clothing, but he couldn't leave her like that for three weeks. So, he had Katrina go out and buy everything he could think of. When Sarah was in the bathroom, David had peeked at the label of Sarah's dress and looked inside her shoes so that he could give Katrina her dress and shoe sizes. He figured Katrina could figure out the rest from there.

Katrina brought brand name jeans, t-shirts, sweatshirts, sweaters, shorts, dresses, skirts, blouses, slacks, shoes, and even under garments. It really was an entire wardrobe. Sarah was surprised and a little shy to accept these gifts, but she was also very grateful. She didn't want to have to leave this place, and the new clothes were a breath of fresh air, as if David was handing her a new lease on life.

After Katrina left, David grilled steaks and poured expensive red wine. Sarah helped prepare the side dishes, and the two of them toasted to new beginnings. Sarah indulged in four glasses of wine with dinner.

After dinner, Sarah and David moved over to the living room to settle in to watch movies. Nestled into the couch, nuzzling and giggling, David and Sarah began making out before they could decide on a movie.

Sarah got on top of David and pressed her body into him hard, taking his mouth with hers, desperate for his kiss. David was surprised by this and was worried the wine was making her frisky. He didn't want to stop her, but he also didn't want to take advantage of her. He kept his hands chaste and only put them on her shoulders and her back. She grabbed his face with one hand as she kissed him more passionately. *"Wow!"* David thought, *"The virgin can take control!"* David lay down on his back, allowing Sarah to lie on top of him, and he let Sarah do what she pleased to him. He figured if he let her be in control, things would stay innocent and he wouldn't have to worry about crossing a line she was uncomfortable with.

When Sarah felt David's erection grow, she reached down and rubbed it through his pants. "Easy now," David said. "Let's not get carried away, Sarah. I don't want to take you further than you are ready to go." Sarah brought her hand back up to his shoulder and stopped kissing him. He was worried he offended her, "Or, whatever you want. I didn't mean to stop you, I was just saying. I only want to go as far as you're comfortable going."

"David, today in the Garden of Eden, walking around your beautiful property, out in the fresh air and the warm sun all day long, I began thinking."

"Yes?"

"I was thinking. I've waited my whole life to have sex. I'm almost 30 years old. Most people are astonished by how long I've waited. The reason I've waited so long is because I wanted to give myself to only one man. I wanted to give myself to my husband on our wedding night. And he was supposed to be the only man who would ever make love to me. But yesterday, when I came so close to losing my virginity to a rapist, I realized. That might not be within my control. If I'm attacked again -- and they say 1 in 4 women suffer a sexual attack at some point in their lives or another, which is a very high risk -- if I'm attacked again, then I would've spent my whole life waiting, only to allow a criminal to steal that from me. I don't want my first sexual experience to be like that. I want to be able to choose who I give my virginity to. I want to give it to a man who deserves me. And you deserve me, David. You're my hero."

David gently took Sarah's face into his hands. He held her there with both hands, as he looked deep into her eyes. "Sarah. I need to know this is real. I can't take your virginity now. Not like this, not while you might still be under the influence of a traumatic experience. When you give yourself to me, I want to know for certain you truly and deeply want to give yourself to me. I want to know that you are not reacting to a traumatic experience. Sarah, we have to wait. It's not time yet. You are safe now. You are in my house. I will not let anyone on these grounds until you say you're ready to leave. You will be protected in my home and under my care for as long as you want to stay here. This is my sanctuary, our sanctuary. You are safe."

Sarah stared deep into David's blue eyes. She felt confused. She already loved this man. She wanted to give herself to this man. He was her hero. She couldn't imagine giving herself to anyone else. Even if they would not end up married one day, this was him. This was the man she had been waiting to give her virginity to her whole life. Sarah didn't speak. She just looked into David's eyes.

David searched Sarah's face for some reaction. He needed to know what she was thinking. So he spoke again. "Sarah, believe me, I want to make love to you. You have no idea how much I want to make love to you, but please, this is very important to me. I want our first moment of love-making to be as special as the night you've always pictured in your mind as your wedding night."

Sarah's face lit up with a bright warm smile. Now, she understood David. He was now wishing to share that moment with her that she had always dreamed of sharing with her future husband on her wedding day. And this made her love David even more. This was the man of her dreams. And she believed, that more than likely, he would be her husband one day. She giggled at the role reversal they had just experienced. Now, she had to be patient with him. She had to wait until he was ready. She had to prove that she genuinely loved him, before they could have sex.

CHAPTER 12

Sarah and David had enjoyed David's sanctuary for about one and half weeks, now. They had explored every part of the grounds. He taught her how to swing a golf club. They played tennis. They swam in his pool. They drank champagne in the jacuzzi on his lower balcony, which overlooked the ocean. They had snuggled on a cozy couch on his upper balcony, watching the sunset over the ocean. And they watched movies together. They watched lots of movies together. Sarah insisted on seeing every one of David's movies. So they snuggled on the couch in his living room. They made popcorn from the popcorn machine in his home movie theatre. They ordered movies from his Blu-ray while lying on his sofa in his den.

They enjoyed each other's company as much as two people could enjoy each other. They had his whole place to themselves uninterrupted. It was like a honeymoon, only without the sex. Sure, they snuggled, they kissed, and they made out. But David had not even put his hands up her shirt or down her pants. He gave her love and affection but would not make any sexual advances. The two of them had never felt so much happiness in all their lives. David and Sarah spent most of their time laughing together. Their chemistry was magical. The happiness was uncontainable.

By this time, enough special moments were shared between them, that the incident that brought them together had long since been forgotten. David and Sarah felt like two lovers who were meant to be. One night in bed, David held Sarah and whispered, "I can't believe how perfect things are between us." Sarah responded, "I think it's because we are meant to be together." And David whispered back, "I know."

Their bond was strong. And today, Sarah wanted to take it to the next level. She had already told David that her favorite place in all the world was his Garden of Eden. So, when she asked him to bring a blanket so that they can spend the day by the waterfall, he thought nothing of it. David laid a thick soft blanket down on the ground and they sat on it. Sarah then removed her shoes and lay down seductively. She sprawled out onto her back, raising her hands above her head. She turned both knees to one side, which emphasized the curve of her body. Her short summer dress moved up her legs as she stretched and moved her curvaceous body. The dress barely covered her bottom now. She began playing with her own hair. David lay down next to her on his side, his head resting on his hand, and he just watched her adoringly. This moment was so special. There she was -- a gorgeous, natural beauty lying in his perfect paradise, nature's beauty surrounding them.

Sarah turned her head towards David and casually, but very naturally, whispered to him, "Make love to me." David's eyes bulged out of his head. "What!?" She smiled warmly. "I think it's time, David. I want to give myself to you." This time, when he heard her ask for sex, it felt right. David leaned in and he kissed Sarah softly on the lips. Then he put one hand gently on the left side of her face, as he slid his lips to her right ear, and whispered, "Are you sure?" Sarah whispered seductively back, "Yes. I'm sure."

David then gently moved on top of her. She wrapped her arms and legs around him, wanting to feel him as close as possible. They kissed passionately. He ran his fingers through her hair. He kissed her neck. He kissed her shoulder. He kissed her right breast through her dress. "Ah!" she whispered, as his lips made contact with her breast. He then slowly caressed her right shoulder and glided his hand toward the same breast, moving his mouth to her left breast. With his right hand, he slipped his finger under the thin fabric of her dress and very softly circled her right nipple with his forefinger, as his mouth closed around her left nipple. Sarah's body arched toward his hand and his mouth, as she sighed with pleasure. He then brought both his hands down the side of her body as he brought his lips up to her mouth, slipping his tongue deep inside her mouth. As he kissed her, his hands reached the hem of her dress and he gently raised her dress up. He lifted his lips off of hers so he could watch as he undressed her. It was like unwrapping the most beautiful gift God ever gave him. He lifted her dress up, and exposed her gorgeous naked breasts. Wow, they were magnificent. He was so glad she wasn't wearing a bra that day. Unveiling those beautiful breasts with just a swift lift of thin fabric was so exhilarating. He swore he could hear angels singing in heaven when he saw her gorgeous breasts. His mouth claimed those breasts desperately. He sucked, he suckled, he licked. She moaned with pleasure. He lifted her dress above her head and tossed it to the side. He moved slightly away from her now so he could take in her beauty. She lay there relaxed and happy with her long, thick dark hair sprawled out around her. Her nearly naked body lying relaxed on the grass, surrounded by the beauty of God's green earth, bright flowers, flowing water, lush vegetation, fluttering butterflies, and birds singing, it was a sight to behold! She had only the smallest pale pink lace panties covering her now.

David took his index finger and lifted and pulled just the middle of the panties down, exposing her femininity where her clitoris was located.

Then he kissed her there. "Oh!" Sarah gasped, breathy and high pitched. He kept kissing her there. As his mouth worked his magic, his hands slid those panties off of her. David kept kissing, and licking and teasing. Her head thrashed from side to side in ecstasy. Her fingers grabbed his hair. His tongue continued its soft but determined assault. Now he brought his fingers up. David lifted his head to watch Sarah, as he began fondling her clit with his finger. Her "Ahs" were louder now, and he continued. He slipped his finger towards the entrance of her vagina, as he kissed her clit, keeping his eyes up so he could watch her. He kissed her clit while he penetrated her vagina with his finger. "Oh!" she shouted. Her back arched, raising her beautiful breasts up. She was so gorgeous. She was so sexy. He loved watching her like this. He knew he was supposed to be making love to her, but he wanted to pleasure her with his hands so he could watch her body move with the pleasure he was giving her.

Her pussy was so tight and so wet. He kept penetrating her with his finger. She was screaming with pleasure. He wouldn't stop. He wanted to make her cum. So he continued pushing his finger in and pulling it out. With every arch of her back and thrust of her head, he penetrated harder and faster. Her breathing became faster and faster, her screams became louder, he knew she was close so he kept on with more determination, until... finally, she came. Her toes pointed, her body tensed; and one long scream of "Aaaaaaahhhhhh!" came out of her mouth, then her body shook a little before she relaxed, and another long feminine sigh escaped her lips. She was lying on her back with her arms spread out and her mouth open. David got on top of her and kissed her. He was so hard now. But he had to give her a minute to collect herself before he would go on to the next phase. He pressed his body against hers, as he kissed her neck. He pressed his cheek against hers and whispered, "I love you Sarah. You are my wife. Right here, right now, I am making you my wife. Never mind the legal paper. We can do that for the world later. But between you and I, today, right now, you are becoming my wife."

Sarah kissed him passionately at the sweet sound of his words, and he knew she was now ready for more. So he kissed her deeply, and with his tongue deep in her throat, his arms holding her tight and her arms wrapped around him, he eased himself into her gently. "Ah!" A quick gasp escaped her.

"Shhh," he said, "I've got you. I won't let go of you." David had barely penetrated the entrance of her vagina, and he felt Sarah tense up. He wanted to relax her, he wasn't even close to her hymen yet, it was just the tip of his penis barely passed the entrance of her vagina. She was still very wet from his digital penetration, which was helpful, but she was a virgin and she instinctively tensed as he began to enter her.

David decided he had to just go for it. He couldn't avoid hurting her when breaking through her hymen, so he had to just do this. He had felt her relax slightly when he told her he'd never let her go, so he looked into her beautiful face and then he thrust one deep thrust into her. As he felt himself break through a barrier, he saw her wince and jerk her head back with a grunt of pain. With his penis all the way inside her now, she grabbed onto him for dear life.

After his first thrust, he left his penis pressed into that spot hoping to ease her pain the way holding a pricked finger helped ease pain. She seemed to relax after a few seconds, so he slid himself outward slightly, then he thrust into her again. He still felt the resistance of her hymen as he broke through the rest of that barrier, and she jerked her head back again with the same grunt of pain. He held his penis there again, not moving, watching her face closely, just waiting for her pain to subside. Then when her face relaxed, he moved outward again and thrust forward. This time there was no resistance and she didn't wince. So he began his steady rhythm. Sarah loved it. "Ooooh" "Ooooh" "That feels so good!" she exclaimed. "I can't believe it, it feels so good!" Her eyes were wide with disbelief as she stared into his face, doe-eyed and full of wonder. David looked into her beautiful eyes and knew, he was introducing her to a whole new world. He never lifted his eyes from her beautiful face as he steadily, made sweet, gentle love to her. His rhythm was slow and gentle. He watched her, as wonder turned to ecstasy. He continued on, hoping she would cum. He wanted to make her cum like this. As he watched her relax and fall deeper into ecstasy, he quickened his rhythm. He kissed her breasts, he kissed her neck. He kissed her lips, and he thrust deep and fast, but not too hard. She kept holding him tight, as she began her loud screams that told him she was getting close again. So he continued, and he continued, and continued,... then finally, he felt her coming all around him. He felt her whole body tense then release as she screamed in ecstasy. Then her body and her grip on him began to relax, so he let himself go, coming deep inside her as she let out one last cry of pleasure.

David laid blissfully on top of Sarah after their mutual orgasm, his arms holding her tight, his face close to hers, whispering to her how much he loved her. Sarah's panting sighs told him she was still coming down off her orgasm, trying to catch her breath. He held her. He kissed her, loved her like that until they fell asleep, still in the same position they were in when he came inside her.

CHAPTER 13

After Sarah had given David her virginity, their bond became so strong, it felt like they were one. He had told her in that moment he took her virginity, that he was making her his wife, and it felt real. It felt like she was now his wife. The two were inseparable. They spent every moment by each other's sides, constantly wrapped in each other's arms, touching at all times. They each had a desperate need to physically feel the other, no matter what activity they were engaged in. They touched each other lovingly, while watching TV, while cooking, while eating, while walking on the beach or walking around David's expansive grounds. They needed to be touching in some way every second of the day. And electricity always fired right through each of them, with every touch and every kiss.

After David broke her seal, Sarah became insatiable. David had given her the most precious experience she could have ever hoped for in giving a man her virginity. He had given her heavenly pleasure, not once, but twice as he pulled her away from her innocence and into his new world. And she needed more. She needed him like he was her drug. For the next few weeks that she remained in his sanctuary, before resuming real life again, they made love three times a day. Each morning began the same;

David would roll over, and gently pull Sarah underneath him as he kissed her good morning. Then their good-morning kiss would roll into sweet lovemaking. Afterwards, they would shower together, then walk down the stairs hand in hand where they cooked together. Sometimes pancakes, sometimes waffles, and sometimes omelets. They would caress each other and kiss each other throughout the preparation of the meal, and sometimes David would lay her down on a nearby couch to give her more love, before they began eating.

David was so impressed at how quickly Sarah accepted her sexuality, and how swiftly she became comfortable with it. But the person David should have been impressed with was himself. It was him who made Sarah so comfortable and so willing. It was his tender love. It was his patience. It was his attentiveness, and skill and selflessness that made Sarah's introduction to sex, so wonderful that she kept seeking more and more. She followed his lead with such grace and beauty as he lead her further and further into a world she'd never known before. He loved showing her all this.

It was now the afternoon of the third day after Sarah had given David her virginity. They had now formed a habit of taking afternoon naps in the nude. They were both awake now and David was caressing Sarah's skin. He could feel her getting frisky and being a little more assertive than she'd been yet. David could tell Sarah was now ready to be on top. So he laid on his back and whispered, "get up there baby." Sarah didn't hesitate. She crawled on top of him, kissing and caressing his chest as she found her position. She was a little awkward at first, trying to find the right position, but David just laid there patiently, letting her feel her way around until she became comfortable and ready to go. She squirmed around on top of him for a little while, but once she found her groove, it was amazing.

David lay on his back completely mesmerized by her. She was now sitting straight up on top of him, rocking up and down, up and down.

The pleasure he felt was out of this world. He couldn't believe it, she was the best sex he'd ever had. He loved the view of her small waist and large breasts rocking above him, as she sat up, riding his manhood. He watched her long black hair fall down her bare skin, whipping around her face and chest, as she thrashed her head around wildly, in ecstasy, loudly screaming a high pitched sound: "Ah! Aaaaaah!" At times her cries of pleasure were shear screams that nearly sounded like cries for help. The erotic dream David had of her the night he first saw her, was now real life. And this was even better than his dream!

David just watched as she moved, her perfect breasts bouncing. Her screams of pleasure so loud, he was afraid his distant neighbors would call the police. But he couldn't interrupt her. He would not try to quiet her. The sound was music to his hears. He just watched in amazement as she took her pleasure from him. He loved watching her unleash years of pent up sexuality. And it was all his. He would make sure he was the only man in the world who would ever have this. He was going to make her his wife.

David loved listening to Sarah's desperate cries for more and more pleasure. And he loved watching her. But he needed her close. "Come here, baby," he whispered. Sarah moved to the sound of his voice, as if it had a natural command over her body. She leaned down, bringing her face close to his, pressing her body against his. He wrapped his arms around her tight, and felt her perfect breasts pressing into his chest. As she rocked into him, her breasts bounced up into his face. Oh, he loved this. This was David's favorite position.

He loved that closeness of heart and soul he felt when they were in that position. He'd never felt that with anyone else before. "Come for me, baby," he whispered. He knew he should've let her go on, but he just had to feel that moment. And again, as if his words commanded her body, she came -- with a screaming, hyperventilating orgasm that sounded as if she would lose her mind if it went on -- her body convulsing with pleasure. God! He loved how he could do that to her! It was the best thrill of all. Just as he felt her body begin to relax and he heard her exhale--that ultra feminine sound, his own release burst inside her. She thrashed her head back and grabbed him tight with both arms, moaning again with more pleasure, her body shaking as she exhaled: "aaaaaahhhhh." He loved to hear and feel her pleasure as he came insider her. He held her closer, squeezing her close to him, with their faces nuzzled against each other.

After holding her in a tight embrace for a while, David began to very, very gently caress Sarah's skin. Her breathing was still heavy. He'd wait for her to catch her breath before he kissed her. He caressed her skin gently. He stroked her long black hair, and whispered breathlessly: "You don't know how much, I love you. I want to marry you." In response, Sarah just hummed with pleasure, "Mmmm." But that was ok with David. He didn't need to hear her repeat his words. He just needed to express his own feelings for her. Also, he had a vague idea from their prior lovemaking, that after she orgasms like that, she can't form words to speak. And that brought a smile to David's face. He figured this is what a woman meant by the phrase, "mind-blowing orgasm." And it was.

CHAPTER 14

For the rest of her life, Sarah would cherish the three weeks she had spent in David's sanctuary. It was a rebuilding and a re-birth for her. And it was the most amazing experience of her life. She hated having to go back to real life today. It was the Monday after her three-week leave of absence, and this morning had to be different from all the lovely mornings she had shared with David during the past three weeks.

This morning, Sarah had to shower alone so things wouldn't evolve and make her late for work. Breakfast was already made when she got downstairs, so she missed out on her treasured morning breakfast preparation that she and David enjoyed together every day for the last three weeks. She kissed him on the lips and thanked him for making breakfast, then she ate quickly before she had to rush off to work.

As David walked her to the front door, with her hand in his, she looked longingly at the couch they frequently made love on between cooking and eating breakfast during the last week or so. She wished she could stay in this fairy-tale forever, but she felt like that wasn't realistic, or wise. Sarah was headstrong. She was not the type to change her whole life after only three weeks of bliss. While her heart and her soul yearned to give everything up so she could be with David full-time, her mind told her no, it was not prudent. And she always followed her mind.

When she hugged and kissed David good-bye that morning, she looked into his sweet face and saw sadness there. His lips were turned down in an almost child-like pout and his eyes were sad. They seemed to turn even bluer with that emotion. It was hard for her to look into those sweet blue eyes and walk out the door. His eyes tugged at her heart. She didn't know why David looked so sad. They had discussed what today would be like. Today, Sarah would go to work, but she would be right back here afterwards, and they had made a commitment to reserve all their evenings for spending quality time together. It wasn't like she was leaving him for good. It was just eight hours, and she'd be back.

But David's heart had a secret desire. He had secretly hoped that he had made Sarah so happy during the past three weeks that she would want to give up her job and marry him. After all, she should be able to see with her own eyes how wealthy he was, how easy and luxurious life could be with him, and that she would never have to work again. But Sarah hadn't even hinted at wanting that, and this made David sad. He didn't know how to ask an accomplished attorney to throw away her life's accomplishments for him. And logically, he knew he shouldn't, but emotionally, he wished she would want to do that on her own. It felt a little bit like she was choosing her job over him. As Sarah kissed him by the front door, David told himself to snap out of these thoughts, because they were absurd. So he forced a smile and told Sarah he hoped she had a good day at work.

On her drive into work, Sarah felt strong and confident and ready to conquer the world. David's love made her strong. The amazing sexual experiences they shared had completely overshadowed and nearly erased the experience White Jr., had exposed her to. It hadn't even crossed her mind to worry about what it would be like to see him in the courthouse. He was nothing. David rendered White Jr., completely insignificant.

White Jr., had failed. Sarah had stayed a virgin through the ordeal and she accomplished her life dream of saving her virginity for a man who would love her and cherish her forever. And she had a more amazing experience than she had ever imagined it would be like, giving her virginity away. It was more romantic than how she'd visualized her wedding night might be. And it was just as special, because David had whispered in her ear, "You are my wife." Those words were everything Sarah needed to hear in that moment. Sarah drew strength from knowing David wanted to marry her. But she assumed, he meant that they would get around to that in the future. It never dawned on her that he meant, let's get married, right now. Sarah believed in making wise, well thought out decisions. She would never run off and get married on a whim. Though she was no longer a virgin, she still held marriage sacred. And marriage was supposed to be forever. She needed to make sure that she and David were compatible all the time, and for an extended period of time, not just when they were honeymooning in his fairy-tale land. And she had to be realistic, three weeks was no time to really get to know someone. It would take at least a year to get to that point, wouldn't it? Sarah's heart and soul disagreed with her mind. Her heart and soul were bonded to David right now and they knew it had to stay that way forever.

Back at the office, it was like Sarah hadn't missed a beat. Her routine came back to her in no time. It was second nature to her. She had a contested hearing today, arguing about the constitutionality of a sentence she was recommending. The court had instructed counsel to brief the issues, which she had done before her leave. She was now reviewing the written arguments of both sides before court. All the arguments she had written three weeks ago were now fresh in her mind, and she was ready to get back into the courtroom and demand the sentence this criminal deserved.

Sarah was successful, as usual. The Court ruled in her favor and followed her recommendation. It was good to be back.

As Sarah turned the corner walking away from the courtroom in which she had just convinced a judge to sentence a man for life, she saw a group of police officers gathered.

"Can you believe that fuck'n defense lawyer!" Sarah heard one of the officers say.

"He gets thrown through a glass window and is laid up in the hospital for weeks, and he won't say who did it!"

Sarah froze. She knew exactly who they were talking about. She stopped within earshot to listen. She held her file folder open, pretending to be concentrating heavily on what was inside. She couldn't let anyone see her face while this topic was being discussed. She listened as the officer went on.

"He's asserting attorney-client privilege! His own client tries to rob him, and this mother fucker asserts attorney-client privilege!"

So that's how White Jr., explained his injuries, Sarah thought. Sick to her stomach with disgust, Sarah couldn't hear anymore. She hurried past the officers.

On her drive home to David, Sarah was remembering what she had overheard the officers say. She wished she hadn't heard them. It brought back the images of that incident. She kept picturing White Jr., hurling through the air and crashing through the glass. He deserved it. He even deserved worse. Now he was trying to make himself out to be some hero defense lawyer who wouldn't turn on his own client, even if he was the victim. It disgusted her to think of how he was getting away with his crime against her. Violent thoughts of more things Sarah thought White Jr., deserved passed through her mind. Hearing the details of how White

Jr., explained himself out of that mess made her sick. She would've rather never heard anything at all.

The only person in the world that she could talk to about how she was feeling, was David. But she didn't want to burden him with it. She didn't want to ruin their happy blissful time together, thinking about that scumbag -- especially now that they had less free time to spend together. She forced thoughts of White Jr., out of her mind, and instead began thinking of what she wanted to cook David for dinner. He was so sweet to make breakfast all by himself. She wanted to nurture him back and make him a nice dinner. But it was hard to do that after working all day long. So she stopped at the grocery store and bought instant biscuits, microwave-ready mashed potatoes, corn on the cob, and salmon. This was a meal she could whip up in 20 minutes.

David laughed at the meal Sarah was making. He was used to the gourmet meals his chefs prepared, but he wasn't going to say that to her. As David laughed while he watched her, Sarah said:

"What?"

And David just laughed without answering.

"What," she demanded, "What's so funny?"

"Nothing. I was just thinking how cute you looked. Are sure you don't need help?"

"No. You made breakfast. I need to make dinner for you."

David chuckled, "Ok. I love you, baby."

"I love you too, David."

"How much more butter are you going to put on that corn on the cob? And why are you cooking it that way? I've never seen my chefs cook it that way."

"Just you wait, David. This is going to be the best corn on the cob you ever tasted."

Sarah was frying the corn on the cob in a frying pan. She just added tons of butter and salt and turned the corn around in the melting butter, letting it burn slightly, darkening the corn. She used tongs to twist the corn as it browned in the butter and salt. She wondered why everyone who saw her cooking this way made fun of her as if they'd never seen such a thing before. It worked and it turned out really good.

When Sarah served dinner, David said, "Thank you, baby." And she said, "You're welcome," and kissed him on the lips. She watched him eating her food, hoping he'd like it.

"Mmm!" he said, "That's so good! You were right, baby, that corn is soo good!"

"Thank you, my love."

"No, I mean it! It's really good!"

Sarah reveled in David's compliment. She loved being able to feed him food he enjoyed. She tried to give him a little more time to finish his food, but she couldn't hold herself back for very long. His sweet happy face melted her heart. She had to go over and kiss him. So she walked over to his side of the table, stood in front of him, and kissed his closed lips while he chewed his food. He smiled. Then she straddled him in his chair and waited for him to swallow what he was chewing. He watched her with a light in his eyes. When he finished his bite, he wrapped his arms around her and they kissed a long, sensuous kiss. He rubbed her bottom and looked in her eyes.

"Baby, I know we've had this place all to ourselves for three weeks, and I love it that way, but do you mind if I bring the staff in tomorrow to help tidy the place up, and maybe give us a day off from cooking?"

Sarah looked at him, her brown eyes round with surprise, "You don't like my food?"

David laughed. "No, no," he said between laughs. "That's not what I meant," he tried to explain, as he kissed her. He kept kissing her between his words, cupping her face in his hands, "That's," mmm, "not," mmm, "what," mmm. "I meant," mmm.

She kissed him back, interrupting his sentence. She shoved her tongue in his mouth, demanding a more passionate kiss, and he gave it to her. Then he tugged at her pants with both hands.

"Take these off," he said.

"No," she said, as she grinded into him, teasing him.

He kissed her some more. Against her mouth he mumbled, "Mmm, take these off!"

"No," she said again, grinding into him more. Then her grind turned into a bounce. She could feel his dick through her pants, getting harder and harder. She wrapped her arms around him tight as she kissed him hard and continued teasing him in his dining room chair, straddled on top of him, grinding and bouncing.

"Grrr," he growled, "I said take them off!"

She bit the side of his jaw gently, then licked him there.

"Oooh, I like that."

"Yeah?"

"Yes, Sarah," he sighed. "Please…. take your pants off," he whispered.

She pressed her lips against his ear, and whispered back: "Ok."

First Sarah fumbled with David's jeans, while she still straddled him, unbuttoning and unzipping his pants, freeing his erection as it sprung out of the opening of his jeans.

"Yes!" she whispered, a breathy, seductive sound. Then she stood in front of David as he reached for her pants, swiftly unbuttoning and unzipping her pants. He yanked them down with her underwear, and demanded: "Now, get back up here." Sarah wiggled her pants the rest of the way off, stepping out of them and back into David's lap. She straddled her man again. She then moved on top of him, slowly and deliberately staring deep into his eyes. And they made sweet, passionate love in his dining room chair.

CHAPTER 15

Over the next few months, David and Sarah continued their bliss. They had quickly gotten back into the groove of everyday life, and did not allow life to interfere with their love. Sarah had kept her commitment to scale back at work so that her evenings remained free for David, even if that meant bringing files home to review and prepare for court while David watched TV. David's Malibu mansion was now home to Sarah. She had spent every single night there since the day he saved her.

Only once did she spend the night in her tiny little one-bedroom apartment in Santa Monica, but David was with her that night. David was curious about where Sarah lived, and she thought it would be fun to spend a cozy evening in her tiny little apartment together. It was cozy and it was fun. David thought it was cute. But he also thought it was smaller than most hotel rooms he usually stayed in, as he always stayed in penthouse suites. So Sarah didn't try to torture him by asking him to spend any more time there, even though Malibu was a farther drive from work. David and Sarah spent every evening in Malibu. And that's the place they both called "home."

It didn't bother David that Sarah would sometimes work at home. She was always by his side when she did it, and it felt the same as if she were just relaxing by his side, reading a novel. In fact, sometimes David would sit next to her and read a novel himself so that the noise of the TV would not disrupt her concentration. To him, it still felt like quality time together. He was happy to simply have her safely at his side. Sarah tried to keep the working from home at a minimum so that she could enjoy her time with David before going to bed. She loved their lively conversations and the fun discussions they would have about any topic a person could discuss. David was more than just an amazing lover and boyfriend; he was great company. There was no one on this earth that Sarah wanted to spend more time with than David. She was happiest when she was by his side. Over these past few months, Sarah and David had quickly become best friends.

Tonight was a weeknight, but they had decided to go out on the town. It was difficult for David to decide where to take Sarah. His biggest fear was that they would, by chance, encounter someone from his old Hollywood lifestyle who would say something that revealed his old play boy ways. David knew he was thought of as a womanizer in Hollywood, though he had always justified it to himself by convincing himself that all his prior women were willing accomplices to his casual trysts. He never thought of it as womanizing because he never led anyone on, and he never made false promises of love or relationship. He was always up front about the lack of commitment and would not get involved with a girl, unless she acknowledged that she was only in it for the good time. He had done this to avoid uncomfortable or complicated situations.

Back then, he thought that was perfectly fine. But now, after he had formed such a beautiful bond with his precious Sarah, that old lifestyle seemed ugly and a little dirty to him now. He would be ashamed if Sarah ever found out that was how he had lived. He was also deathly afraid that she would never accept it and would leave him if she learned too much about his old ways. So, David was always very cautious to keep Sarah away from Hollywood.

In fact, she had never seen or even heard of his party house in the Hollywood Hills. He hadn't been there in months - not since the day he rescued Sarah. His house in the Hollywood Hills was now empty, except for the permanent staff that manned the place -- one butler, one maid, and one full-time Chef -- all just standing by waiting to be of use. Of course, during his parties, he would have added staff for each event, but for day-to-day operations, it was just the three people who made up his permanent staff in his Hollywood home.

Although David had considered updating his Facebook status to indicate he was in a serious relationship, he was also afraid that a jealous ex-lover might seek out Sarah and ruin their relationship. So, he did not update Facebook and he did not post pictures of himself and Sarah anywhere on Facebook. He was happy that Sarah had always been too busy to bother having a Facebook account of her own, so the subject would never come up.

Tonight, David asked Sarah: "Do you want to go to Geoffries, baby?"

Sarah answered: "No, I think I'm getting bored of that place."

"But you love Geoffries. It's romantic, it's right on the ocean, great food, great service."

"I know. I still love that place, but I kind of feel cooped up. We always stay in Malibu. I feel like venturing out."

"But it's a week night baby. I don't want you to be tired for work tomorrow."

"I don't have court. It's just going to be deskwork tomorrow. So it's a good night to go out. Can we go into Hollywood?"

"No, baby!"

"Why not?"

"Umm, uh, it's too far."

"It's not that far."

"Baby, it's already dark. I don't feel like driving that far. Aren't you tired from your drive from work? Do you really want to get back into the car and drive at least another half hour, probably 45 minutes?"

"Gosh, baby, you're such a slow driver. I could get into Hollywood from here faster than that."

"No, you can't!" he argued with a smile.

"Yes, I can!" she insisted, with her own smile.

"Baby, that's dangerous. Please don't ever drive that fast in this area."

Sarah then kissed David's lips. She thought he was so sweet to worry like that. David viewed her kiss as an opportunity -- maybe he could distract her, he thought. So David kissed Sarah more deeply. He put his right hand on the back of her head and held her against him. Then, with his left hand, he began pulling at her blouse, trying to untuck it out of her pants. Sarah swatted David's hand away.

"No, baby. I want to go out," she said.

"Don't deny me Sarah. I'm a hungry man," he said, as his left hand returned to her blouse, pulling more assertively, he quickly slipped his hand beneath her blouse. Gliding his hand up the side of her waist, he stopped at her breast and gave it a gentle squeeze, then he began very softly massaging her breast, his thumb pressing into her nipple, then circling around it.

His swift hands were too fast, too smooth, he had reached and triggered Sarah's erogenous zone before she could resist him again. She sighed with a gentle "ah," closing her eyes, tilting her head back, opening her mouth and pressing her breast into his hand, as if begging for more. David looked into to her gorgeous face, then claimed her mouth with his own as he continued working her breast. He was going to kiss her and caress her until she forgot all about Hollywood.

Sarah and David forgot to eat dinner that night. The more Sarah would try to say, between kisses, "we should get going," the more David would lay on the pleasure. She was his prisoner. His hands entrapped her with the pleasure they delivered, and Sarah gave herself up to David that night, over and over again, until they fell asleep without dinner.

The next afternoon, while Sarah was at work, David had lunch with Frank. Frank was his good friend who always had sage advice. So David asked Frank what he should do about his predicament.

"Well David, you can't keep her out of Hollywood forever."

"I know, Frank, but what should I do?"

"You have to sit her down one day and explain things to her."

"But how? How do I start that conversation?"

"You just say, 'I want you to know, I am fully committed to you and wouldn't change that for the world, but I want to let you know, I wasn't always this way,...' and you take it from there."

"So how do I explain the, 'I wasn't always this way' part? Do I say, 'I used to be a no-good son-of-a-bitch who used to take two or three women into his bedroom at a time?'"

"You should probably start out a little softer than that."

"Like how. What do I say?"

"Maybe you say, 'My lifestyle was a little looser than it is now that I've found the woman I'm meant to be with for the rest of my life.'"

"Then she'll ask, 'looser how, what does that mean...'"

"Look David. You just have to trust yourself that you'll find the right words. And you have to trust that she'll forgive you. I mean it was the past, how can she judge you for what you did before you knew her?"

"She's really conservative, Frank. I mean really conservative." David never told Frank that Sarah was a virgin when he met her. He didn't think it was anyone's business. Sarah's virginity was her precious gift to

David. And part of keeping it to himself was to not talk about it to anyone, but to simply treasure that intimate moment between him and Sarah in his own private thoughts.

"David. You have to trust her. If she loves you, she'll forgive you, no matter what you've done in your past."

"Can I wait to trust her until after she marries me?"

"I don't know buddy, you're taking a bigger risk there."

"Why, she won't leave me for something like that, after we're married."

"Then, why do you think she'll leave you for something like that, now?"

"My fear is that a girl like her would never want to marry a guy with my past. But I know once she is married, she'll be committed."

"So, you plan on keeping the lifestyle you had just a few months ago, a complete secret from her until after she's trapped in a marriage with you?"

"Ha, ha," David chuckled at his friend's characterization of David's plan. "Why do you have to call it trapped? I think she'll like being married to me very much. I just have to get her there."

"David, if you do that, she'll feel like you kept a big bad secret from her, and that will create distrust. Also, what if she finds out through someone else first? You don't know how long it's going to take to get her to the alter and make it official. What if someone beats you to it? You need to make sure she hears it from you first."

"I guess that makes sense. I just need a little more time. I'm not ready to expose her to my old Hollywood lifestyle just yet."

"So, David, speaking of this marriage thing, have you spoken to an attorney about a pre-nuptial agreement, yet?"

"No."

"Are you going to?"

"No."

"Why not?"

"It's not necessary, Frank."

"What do you mean, it's not necessary! Of course it's necessary!"

"Frank, I said it's not necessary. I don't want to discuss this any further."

David was a self-made millionaire. He built himself up to what he was today making his own decisions and using his own intelligence. He found his success going against the grain. He did not take the Ivy League education that was handed to him and was supposed to pave him an easy path to success. He rolled the dice on something that granted him exponentially far greater wealth than what traveling down that paved road would have brought him. His intelligence was life-taught. It wasn't something he learned at an expensive college. And David didn't need anyone telling him what to do. So he abruptly ended the conversation with Frank about pre-nuptial agreements. He would have none of it. He especially was not going to take anyone else's opinion when it came to Sarah. Deep in his soul, David knew he and Sarah would spend the rest of their lives together. This feeling that bonded them was far stronger than anything he could have imagined. He knew Sarah was his soul mate. No matter how long it took to get her to the alter, once they got married, they would stay married, forever. He had no doubt about that. And he was not going to let anything ruin that, not cold business-like negotiations over a pre-nuptial agreement; and not warnings from disbelieving friends who could not understand the bond David and Sarah shared.

CHAPTER 16

It was a typical weekday morning, requiring Sarah to rush through breakfast. As Sarah bit into her toast and reached for her orange juice, David's phone buzzed on the table. She saw a text message appear: "Happy Birthday!" Katrina wrote. The words surprised Sarah:

"Birthday? David, today's you're birthday?"

David smiled shyly, "Yeah."

"Why didn't you tell me?"

"It's not a big deal."

"Of course it's a big deal! I would've stayed home from work, I would've spent the day with you! Oh, David, why didn't you tell me?"

David smiled. He liked that idea. "So just call in sick."

"Oh, my love, I can't. I'm due in court in an hour, and there's no way I can ask someone to cover on such short notice."

David's face fell and Sarah's heart saddened. She hated having to leave him on his birthday.

"I wish you would've told me, then I could've planned for it. Baby, my job is very demanding. I can't just not show up. I have to plan in advance, reschedule hearings, find coverage. It's a lot for me to try to take any time off."

"I understand, Sarah. It's ok."

"Baby, I'll come home as early as I can, as soon as my last court appearance is over. Ok?"

David smiled, "Ok."

"What do you want to do for your birthday, David? It's your day, and I want to make it perfect for you."

David had spent too many birthdays past throwing wild parties in his home in the Hollywood Hills before he met Sarah. This year, all he wanted to do was stay home and enjoy his private time with Sarah. So he said:

"Really, Sarah, the best birthday gift you could give me would be to come home early and just snuggle on the couch with me and watch TV."

"Then I'll come home to you as soon as I can. I should be back by 1:00. I love you David. I'll see you soon."

Sarah kissed David on the lips and rushed off to work.

That afternoon, after court, Sarah had brought home a birthday cake, candles and champagne. She sat in David's lap and sang him a birthday song in his ear. As he blew out the candles, David wished Sarah would quit her job to marry him and have his babies sooner, rather than later. After enjoying their private birthday celebration Sarah and David moved over to the couch to watch TV.

David had the remote control and he was trying to decide what movie to watch. Sarah sat behind him on his extra wide, plush couch that he bought specifically for an occasion like this, to cozy up with her while watching movies. Sarah's legs were wrapped around David and her hands were on his chest. She gripped him firmly with her arms and her legs, and pressed her soft natural breasts into his back. He loved the way that felt. She kissed his neck now and a sweet, masculine sigh escaped him. *"He likes that!"* Sarah thought. And she gave him some more. David loved the feel of Sarah's soft lips on his neck. Somehow her kiss sent an electric wave down to his groin, waking him up down there. With each kiss, David sighed with pleasure. Sarah caressed his chest through his thin t-shirt, then began sliding one hand down. She still held him tight against her, as her hand worked its way down to his pants. She slipped her fingers under his pants and worked her fingertips beneath his underwear until her hand was fully immersed and she wrapped it around what she was looking for.

At first, with feather-light fingers almost tickling him, she gently wrapped her hand around his large, hard erection. Then she squeezed her hand hard around him and held him for a second before she began to rub. "Oh, Sarah," he sighed, "That feels good." She kept kissing his neck, caressing his chest, and rubbing his erection. He loved the sensations he felt all over his body. She rubbed him up and down now, up and down, never loosening her tight grip. Her movement began slow and soft, then gradually became slightly harder and faster. As she gradually picked up speed, his breathing picked up with it, matching the movement of her hand tugging his manhood. She began yanking him hard and his breathing became heavier. She yanked and yanked, his pleasure growing higher and higher. "No, Sarah. Don't make me come, I want to make you come first." But Sarah didn't stop. It was his birthday, and his dick was in her hand. She was in control and she was going to make her man come. She wanted to give him pleasure. She wanted him to relax in her arms, while *she* gave to *him*. "Oh, oh" he said in ecstasy, as she continued jerking her hand up and down relentlessly. "No, Sarah, stop." He warred with himself between enjoying the sensation and wanting to please her first. But Sarah kept jerking her hand up and down, harder and faster, squeezing her breasts into him, kissing his neck, jerking his penis up and down, faster and faster and faster, until... "Oh!" he moaned,... and finally, he came into her hands: "Ohhhh Ohhh, Oh Sarah, I love you. Oh! I love you."

Sarah kept her hand wrapped around David's dick, feeling his pleasure spill over the top of her fist. She kept rubbing his cock, gradually slowing her pace. She loved him so much; she loved feeling his ecstasy release into her hands. She would not remove her sensuous grip. She wanted to get every drop of pleasure out of him. As she continued stroking him, a little more cum came out, and she pressed her lips against his ear and whispered with a hum, "Happy birthday, my love. Happy birthday," as her strokes grew slower and softer, never releasing him before she felt him go soft in her hands. David's head was tilted back with satisfied pleasure showing in his face. He relaxed against her. She could reach his cheek and his lips now; so, she kissed his cheek, then his lips with her hand still gently holding his beautiful cock, now soft in her hands. Her touch became feather light again. God! How he loved her touch! He could feel the love in her hands when she touched him. It was electrifying, even now as he lay against her, satisfied.

Sarah whispered in David's ear, "I love you." David whispered back, "I love you, too." Sarah held him that way for a while, enjoying the sweet look of bliss on his face. She let him rest for a while, but she was aching with desire between her legs. Having held his hard dick in her hand, and feeling his cum spill into her hands, she felt so aroused now; it was almost painful. So when David whispered, "Sarah, why did you make me come, you know I always want to make you come first," Sarah slipped out from behind David, climbed on top of him to face him, straddled him, and said, "Now it's my turn."

David smiled with the slightest hint of exasperation; and while still trying to catch his breath, he said: "Just give me 5 minutes, and I promise I'll be ready again."

Sarah kissed him on the lips. "Don't worry, I can wait."

"No really, it will only take me 5 minutes."

"Ok," she smiled, seductively.

Sarah held David and kissed him. He rubbed his hands up and down her body. They kissed and caressed each other for what only felt like 1 minute, then David was hard again. "I'm ready," he said through one of his kisses. Sarah then stood in front of him, less than an inch away and lifted off her shirt. He watched. She slowly removed her bra. He smiled. She slowly unzipped her pants. He quickly unzipped his. Still seated on the couch and watching her, David slipped off his pants and underwear, exposing his large cock, which now stood straight up ready for her. She removed her pants and lace underwear, then stood in front of him, completely naked. "Wow!" he whispered. "Take off your shirt too," she demanded. He did as he was told, then she climbed back into his lap, looking deep into his eyes. Sarah eased herself on top of him, and they both exhaled with an "awww" as the electricity of that initial contact sent pleasure waves rushing through each of them. Her mouth open, her eyes shutting halfway, Sarah tilted her head back slightly. David watched her with love in his eyes. She then reached for him and the two of them embraced, as Sarah began to ride him. She pressed her face into his and rode him deep and hard.

Then she began to bounce. She lifted her breasts up and began bouncing and bouncing, causing her breasts to fly up and down in his face, she began screaming with pleasure, her screams of pleasure heightening his arousal. He tried to catch her breasts with his mouth as they bounced up and down in his face. He burrowed his face between her breasts, as she bounced, and bounced. He lifted his head up to watch her as she screamed louder and louder. Her screams were a long high-pitched feminine sound, letting out the sound "Aaaaaahhhh" in a long drawn out song. It was as if she was singing him the opera as she bounced on his cock. He loved every minute of it.

The faster and harder she bounced, the louder and more desperate her song became. It was raising his pleasure to such heights that he was worried he would come again, but he held back, he had to let her come first. He struggled to hold back his own pleasure as she continued her wild, uncontrollable bouncing, screaming and thrashing her head around. She grabbed his hair now, and shoved her body hard onto his cock, she almost made him come, so he picked her up and rolled her over, laying her down on the couch beneath him, to regain his control. He pressed his body against her and shoved himself inside her, kissing her neck and her breasts, as he pounded deep inside her with sweet, passionate sensuality matching how desperately she had shoved herself on top of him. He thrust inside her, hard, as she screamed with pleasure: "Ah! Ah! Aaaah! Ah!"

David could feel she was about to come, he just had to hold his pleasure back and wait for her, just a little longer,.... then, finally she let out the highest pitched song he had ever heard, escaping her open mouth. Then she relaxed beneath him, as if she lost all her strength and that's when he let himself go. He came, and came, and came inside her. It seemed to go on a long time. She sang in his ear again, "Aaah," a softer breathless sound, this time, as she felt his come fill her up. It was the most beautiful sound he'd ever heard.

Her face was pressed close to his and they held each other tight. He loved the feel of her body so relaxed underneath him. He could feel in the looseness of her limbs, that her orgasm had been powerful. He put his hand in her hair and whispered in her ear, "you don't know how much I love you, Sarah."

CHAPTER 17

Within just a few weeks after David's birthday, David and Sarah celebrated two major holidays, first Christmas, then New Year's Eve. Christmas was more of a stressful event than a joyous event because in order to spend that time together, Sarah and David were forced to introduce each other to their families. They had been dating long enough that it was time, but still, meeting families for the first time was nerve-racking.

They spent Christmas Day on Skype with Sarah's family from out of state. Because Sarah had to work the day after Christmas, they couldn't go visit, so David had connected his computer to his large screen TV in the living room, to make it feel as if Sarah's family were in the room with them. They met David, caught up with Sarah, and exchanged Merry Christmas greetings. Sarah's family was intrigued with David. Her father inquired about David's work, more interested in his Wall Street days than in his Hollywood days. Everyone else was interested in David's current business: "Which movies have you made?" "Have you met real celebrities?" "Were they cool?" The questions went on. David happily answered their eager questions with a warm smile and the patience of a saint. It was a lovely day, spent mostly on the couch in front of the screen. Sarah got to watch all her nieces and nephews open their gifts, including the ones David and Sarah had sent. David and Sarah sat on their living room couch watching it all transpire on the screen. Each of Sarah's nieces and nephews thanked them and blew them kisses. David's eyes lit up with happiness watching the cute little kids squealing with excitement as they opened gifts. Sarah's youngest nephew was five years old. As he looked at David and Sarah sitting on the couch with David's arm around Sarah, the little boy asked David: "Are you my uncle?" Everyone laughed, and David answered with one word: "Yes."

The night before was Christmas Eve. They had spent Christmas Eve at David's mother's house where Sarah was surrounded by inquisitive family members. David had made sure to adorn Sarah in the finest clothing and jewelry from Rodeo Drive, so that he could show her off in her best light. Sarah proudly wore the new clothes David bought her because she wanted to make him happy. David had a personal shopper who took care of his own clothing, but when it came to Sarah, David decided to go into the store himself to pick out a dress and jewelry, for an occasion as special as this. He looked for something that made him think of Sarah, and he picked the item that best fit the occasion.

For Christmas Eve, David had picked out a conservative long-sleeved dress that was the perfect color red for Christmas. It was made of a thin material that clung close to Sarah's body so that it would emphasize her beautiful shape, though it did not reveal any skin. It sparkled with just the right amount of fine crystals to keep the dress festive but not obnoxious. It was elegant.

The lady at the store explained that because the neck was high, it should not be worn with a necklace, but that large diamond stud earrings would complement the dress nicely, and maybe a diamond bracelet too. So David bought both. He also bought high-heeled open-toed shoes, made entirely of straps lined with diamonds. He had shown the dress to an expensive store a few doors down and the lady there told him these shoes were made for that dress. So he bought the shoes too.

David laughed at himself as he walked down the street to his car, with shopping bags from women's retail stores in his hands, and he wondered to himself: "How did I become *that* guy." But he didn't care. He loved Sarah and he wanted to shower her with the finest things money could buy; and the day he introduced her to his family was a day far too special for him to delegate this duty to staff.

When David surprised Sarah with an entire outfit he had picked out himself for her to wear for Christmas Eve, she was so excited, she kissed him all over. She was so touched by the thoughtfulness and the effort he put in to selecting the perfect thing for her to wear. She was also very pleased that he had done such a good job in his selection. David ate up the attention and savored every kiss she gave him in thanks of the sweet gesture.

David had never had a girlfriend serious enough to take home for Christmas Eve. David's mother, Joy, couldn't believe her son had finally found a girl he wanted to settle down with. And this girl was a smart, well accomplished, respectable, Deputy District Attorney, with very good manners and elegant grace. Joy couldn't believe it. She had always expected David to bring home someone from the entertainment industry, someone more superficial and less educated, a wannabe actress or something. She had never expected or dared hope for this. His mother was more nervous than Sarah. The thing that made her most nervous was the fear that David's wild ways would drive the girl away, so Joy tried to overcompensate for what she feared her son might do in the future.

David's mother, Joy, was pure sweetness and charm. She buzzed around Sarah like an excited bumblebee and doted on Sarah like she was her long-lost daughter. David's eyes sparkled when he watched his mother interact with Sarah. He knew he found someone that made his mother proud, and this filled his heart with overwhelming joy and happiness. It was the best Christmas gift David could hope for.

Throughout the evening, Joy kept asking Sarah, "Are you comfortable, dear?" "Do you have everything you need, darling?" "I want you to be as comfortable in my home as you would be in yours." Joy also took a protective role over Sarah. She felt that all the questions from David's siblings and other family members were putting Sarah on the spot. So Joy would interrupt and shoo them away, "Not so many questions, Tom, it's Christmas Eve, let her enjoy the evening." The whole family was intrigued with Sarah. Not only because she was the first girl David brought home for a special occasion, but also because she was a Deputy District Attorney. They couldn't stop asking about her job.

David's little sister asked, "Have you ever seen a real murderer?"

Sarah answered, "Yes, they have to appear in court for their cases."

Then of course, the whole family bombarded Sarah with questions about her work, "what's the most interesting case you've ever worked on?" "What's the scariest case you've ever worked on." The list of questions went on. Finally, David's mother had to create a rule that nobody was allowed to ask Sarah about her job, because it was Christmas Eve and nobody should be required to think about work on Christmas Eve. She then declared that dinner was ready and the family moved into the dining room for an amazing dinner prepared by Joy, lots of red wine, and even more amazing desserts prepared by Joy. Sarah helped clear the table and Joy thanked her. Then after a final nightcap, David told his mother that he and Sarah needed to get going. They said their goodbyes and drove back to Malibu around midnight, where David and Sarah could finally spend a little Christmas Eve to themselves.

On the drive home, Sarah told David what a lovely family he had and he smiled at her warmly and thanked her.

"I'm glad you liked them, Sarah. I know they all loved you."

Sarah smiled back at him and said: "Merry Christmas, David. I love you."

"Merry Christmas," David said, as he reached for Sarah's hand without taking his eyes off the road. He pulled her hand to his mouth for a sweet gentle kiss.

When David and Sarah got home, David asked Sarah if she would open one of her gifts early. He said it was something he hoped she would wear for him tonight, "with nothing else." The box was very small so Sarah assumed it was a tiny bit of lingerie. But when she opened the box, her eyes widened and her mouth dropped in awe of what she saw. It was the most dazzling, sexy, very expensive-looking jewelry she had ever seen in person. It was a giant, three-tiered diamond necklace that was meant to be worn as body-art between the neck and the hips. She kissed David on the lips and he begged her to put it on now.

"I'll be right back, my love."

"Change in our bathroom, Sarah, I'll wait for you in our bed," David said.

David and Sarah walked hand in hand up the stairs, anticipation rising in each of them.

In their master bath, Sarah stripped nude but left on her strappy diamond shoes. She then began to drape the magnificent diamond body art over her nude body. Her hair and makeup were still perfect from being dressed up for the evening. And now, she would dress in strings of diamonds for David, who was anxiously waiting for her in their bed. The first layer of the giant necklace was a chain of diamonds that wrapped around her neck, with larger diamonds dipping off the chain, much like the charms of a charm bracelet, giving the effect of ice-cycles, sparkling down her chest. The top layer was connected with a string of diamonds that dropped straight down her sternum, separating just below her breasts, diverting in opposite directions to cup around the lower part of each of her large breasts and reconnecting at the top with the first layer. Her voluptuous nude breasts were framed and dazzled with diamonds. And for an extra tease, the third layer was connected with another string of diamonds dropping straight down past her belly button, connecting with the third layer, which landed at the top of what would have been the hairline of her shaved vagina. It wrapped around her hips, connecting with a clasp in the back.

Now, dressed in nothing but strings of diamonds from head to toe, framing her nudity, Sarah slowly walked out of the master bath towards David. He sat up in bed, leaning against the headboard. He looked past the foot of his bed, staring at Sarah, who stood a good distance away, as his master bedroom was very large.

Sarah knew it was the thrill of seeing her like this that was going to turn David on the most. So she took her time. She paused in the doorway of the master bath and let him stare before she began to move. Then, looking into his eyes, she took each step, slowly, one foot at a time, her hips gently swinging with each careful step, as she walked towards him. He watched her, his eyes wide and his mouth open in awe of the beauty before him. When she reached the foot of the bed, she slowly climbed onto the bed, one knee at a time. She stopped there, and sat straight up high on her knees. She stretched her arms up and ran her fingers through her hair. David waited, immobile, as he watched, mesmerized by her. She continued playing with her hair and arching her back in seductive movement to prolong the show.

David watched in silence. She then slowly crawled towards him, across the bed. He didn't move. He just watched. As she reached him, she slid her hands up his legs, slowly caressing him from his ankles to his knees, then his thighs as she moved her body closer towards him, until her pelvis reached his lap. She sat up straight in front of him and slid her vagina over his hard, erect cock. She kept her body straight up so David could enjoy the view of his Christmas gift, while she rocked him -- her sparkling, dazzling body only inches from his face now. The sensations David felt were out of this world. The view of her gorgeous nude body, dazzled with diamonds, her soft breasts bouncing so close to his face, her wet vagina surrounding his hard cock, combining the pleasure of his eyes with the pleasure of his body. David continued watching Sarah as she rocked him, her eyes never leaving his face, his eyes devouring every bit of her magnificent display.

David couldn't take his eyes off of Sarah as she rocked him. His gorgeous blue eyes still wide in awe of the sight of her. He watched her, as he let her have his cock. He was captivated by the jewelry adorning and framing her gorgeous breasts, as he felt the pleasure of her vagina surrounding his hard cock. It felt like a dream. They hadn't spoken. She had just walked towards him in silence, inching closer and closer until she reached his legs, then his groin, then began rocking him into the night.

Still rocking him, now, Sarah grabbed onto the head board with both hands, pressing her breasts into David's face, as her movement on top of him intensified. Finally, the two of them made sound. Loud moans of pleasure escaped both their lips. They held each other tight as Sarah kept rocking David. "Oh, Sarah! Oh God, Sarah!" "Yes, Sarah, Yes!" David shouted. "Aaaah!" "Aaah!" Sarah responded. "Ah! Ah! Aaaah!" she yelled with her own pleasure. "Yes, Sarah, I love you!" David exclaimed. She kept rocking him and loving him, her arms wrapped tight around his neck, his head buried into her soft breasts.

As he tilted his up to look at her face, his deep-blue eyes meeting her passionate brown eyes, David professed his love for Sarah, and they both came, wrapping their arms around each other tighter, kissing passionately as he filled her up with his cum. Then they both fell against the mattress together, where they cooed at each other, and kissed each other until they fell asleep, still wrapped in each other's arms the way they had fallen in orgasm.

CHAPTER 18

A week later, Sarah was in the same master bath getting ready for New Year's Eve. David had surprised her with another dress, and this one was so exciting! Sarah couldn't wait to put it on. She had a staff of hair and makeup people working on her now, making her the perfect beauty for David to display on his arm at the elegant New Year's Eve party he was taking her to tonight. Sarah was thrilled and excited. She imagined this is how a girl felt on her wedding day, being tended to and pampered and prepared for the utmost elegance. She couldn't wait to spend this special evening with David.

She had no idea that David hated New Year's Eve. It was the night his father died. It would always be the night his father died. He could never view it as a day to celebrate. In the past, he could never enjoy the celebrations, but he had gone because he had to go. Parties were a part of the lifestyle. So he would make an appearance, make his rounds and go through the motions, but he would always try to slip out of the party and be outside in a car already before the countdown. The countdown was always the worst part. It always brought back the memory of those two officers standing at the door when he was child, delivering the news of his father's death. He had never taken a date to any New Year's Eve parties before, so that he could slip out before midnight undetected.

But tonight was different. Tonight, he was with Sarah. And he had to hold strong for her. He couldn't bailout this time. He would have to endure the misery of the moment because he did not want to ruin Sarah's evening. He had bought her an elegant designer dress for the evening because he wanted the woman he loved to be as gorgeous as she could be. He surprised Sarah with the dress, which perfectly fit her body. She looked elegant and stunning. The dress was a mix of vibrant colors and dazzling crystal. It hugged every curve of her body, and cinched in tight around her little waist, which emphasized her large breasts, curvy hips, and round bottom. It hugged her thighs and narrowed with the curve her legs, stopping mid-way past the knee. The neckline plunged low, exposing her cleavage. The top of her large breasts protruded so far upward and out of the dress, they threatened to expose nipple. But the dress fit so perfectly, that exposing nipple was not a real risk because the fabric would not move from its firm grip around her voluptuous breasts.

David watched Sarah walk out of the bedroom after she was dressed, and the hair and makeup team that his assistant had arranged for, finished their final touches. First David's mouth dropped, almost hitting the floor. Then he just stared at her with complete adoration. She was so gorgeous he couldn't believe his eyes. David wished they didn't have to go out. He wanted her here, like this, all to himself. But he knew how excited Sarah had been to celebrate New Year's Eve. So he gave her his arm and said: "Shall we?" Sarah took his arm and kissed him on the lips, "Yes. Please." David had been so mesmerized by Sarah's appearance that he actually forgot to compliment her. That didn't bother Sarah, though; because she could see it in his eyes.

The limo drove Sarah and David from his Malibu mansion to the Montage Hotel in Beverly Hills. The ballroom that evening was featuring a gala with a 7 course meal, pairing each dish with the perfect beverage that complimented each plate--one was a fine white wine, the next expensive cognac, the next a fine Champagne, and with dessert, a smooth red wine. The room was decorated with elegance and splendor. Crystal chandeliers hung from the ceiling, fine china and real silver adorned the table. The live band was perfectly pitched at a perfect volume, loud enough to make you want to dance, but not so loud it burst your eardrums. It all made Sarah so happy. This, she thought, is how New Year's Eve should be celebrated! They toasted to their relationship and to more good times to come. They danced, they laughed, they ate and drank and enjoyed the evening as much as possible. As midnight approached, they took to the dance floor like everyone else about five minutes before the countdown.

But as the countdown began, an image of the two police officers flashed in David's mind. Suddenly, he was overwhelmed with sadness. Sarah watched as the smile fell from David's face and sadness appeared in his eyes. She could see that something suddenly triggered a change in his feelings. She didn't know what made David sad, and she was not going to force the subject. All she wanted was to comfort him.

Sarah leaned in and whispered in his ear: "I love you, David." His smile returned to his face, and his eyes lit up as the warmth of her words reached his heart. She looked deep into his eyes, smiling with love and she repeated her words again: "I love you, David."

Looking into Sarah's face, David now felt the brightness of the future. She was his future. She could release the pain in his heart and give him something to look forward to. The strong mix of emotions made one tear fall from David's left eye, as he smiled with warmth and love at Sarah. He didn't wipe the tear away because he did not want to draw attention to it. Sarah kissed the cheek his tear landed on, then kissed his lips. He wrapped his arms around her and they held each other in a warm embrace as they indulged in a long, deep passionate kiss, as the crowd around them roared: "Happy New Year!"

David and Sarah's passionate kiss on the dance floor continued on as the noisemakers sounded all around them and confetti fell from the ceiling. Then David dipped Sarah, and the people around them cheered. He ran his fingers through her hair, firmly but gently, grabbing a chunk of her hair with a clenched fist. Lifting is lips away from her, he gently used his grip to tilt her head back, forcing her chin up in a seductive pose. He looked into her eyes, then kissed her again. He rubbed his check against hers and whispered in her ear: "I think it's time for us to go home, now."

At home, Sarah and David made passionate love all night long.

On New Year's Day, David and Sarah woke up and continued their lovemaking, well into the late afternoon. It was almost dark before they got out of bed for their first meal. It was a beautiful way to start the new year.

CHAPTER 19

As time went on, David and Sarah continued spending all their free time together. Sarah was David's top priority. He would make sure all his business meetings happened during the business day while she was at the office so that his evenings would remain free for her. And Sarah had scaled back at work, leaving the office at 6:00 p.m. whenever she could, but never later than 8:00 p.m. so she could protect her precious evenings with David.

If David ever had to meet a business associate on the golf course on a Sunday, he would bring Sarah along. Sometimes she would lunch with friends at the country club he was golfing at that day, and sometimes she would join him and his company on the course. He taught her to be a good caddy so that having his girlfriend in attendance would blend in naturally with the scene. She wouldn't carry his heavy golf bag, of course, but she was in charge of keeping the beers cold and passing them out. She happily played this role because she loved spending time with David.

David had selected the cute golf clothing he bought her, always putting her in short skirts and tight sweaters so as to show off her beautiful body. Although he loved and respected Sarah, he still wanted to show off her beauty and maintain his status. He had a woman he could be proud of in every way, physically, mentally and spiritually. David loved this about Sarah as much as he loved the fact that she was fun with a sweet bubbly personality, as bright as the sun.

Sarah never let David see her in the courtroom because that was a place that called out more masculine qualities, requiring her to be tough and intimidating. She never showed David that side of her. She wanted David to know the person she was underneath all the tough D.A. bravado, which was necessary for her work but not suitable for romance. Sarah wanted David to know her natural personality, instead -- the one her friends and family from her small town knew. And David loved that Sarah -- more than life itself.

On the golf course today, as his business associate swung his golf club, David watched Sarah sitting in the golf cart. He imagined three children sitting in the golf cart with her. He couldn't wait to have family day out on the course, on a bright sunny day, like today. He pictured a beautiful little girl with Sarah's face and brown hair. He wondered what their children would be like. Would they be little rascals, like himself, wreaking havoc all over the place, but making life so much fun? Or would they be prim and proper like Sarah? He chuckled at the thought as he watched Sarah beaming at him with her beautiful smile, as if she could read his thoughts.

"A hole in one!" his colleague shouted, drawing David out of his fantasy world and back to reality.

"No way! I've never seen anyone do that at this hole! How'd you do that, you S.O.B.!" David bantered back.

"See, I told you!" his business associate said. "You're buying the rounds today! I earned it!"

David looked down and kicked the grass. He didn't mind buying the rounds, but he hated losing at golf.

"David! You be a good sport!" Sarah shouted.

And they all laughed and carried on, enjoying the rest of the day.

After David and Sarah finished their game of golf and the round of drinks David owed his business associate, David drove Sarah straight home. It was Sunday, which meant tomorrow was Monday, which meant he would have precious little time with Sarah for the next five days. So, David wanted to take her home and make love to her for the rest of the afternoon and the evening. When ordering drinks, he had ordered her margaritas because he knew what Tequila did to her, and he liked it. Now, she was squirming in his passenger seat, hands all over him while he drove. David sped down Pacific Coast Highway, his Lamborghini engine roaring as fiery as his libido was roared. He knew Sarah was ready to go!

The next morning, Sarah lay in bed next to David, exhausted from the sexual marathon they indulged in the night before. Lying next to him, turned her on so much. It was frustrating. She wanted more sex, but she was too raw between her legs from the night before, and she was still too dry for sex. David stirred. Awake now, he turned to her and gently and seductively pulled her underneath him, the same way he did first thing every morning. She loved these moments. It was a good-morning kiss that involved their whole bodies. It was filled with passion and love and always naturally evolved into lovemaking.

David was on top of Sarah now, his amazing blue eyes looking into her adoring face. She melted. She needed this man so badly. She could never deny him his sexual desires. She couldn't tell him she was too raw for sex. She didn't want to break that beautiful bond they shared during their special good-morning kiss. But as David eased into her, she could feel pain. She could only bear a few thrusts before she gently whispered: "Baby, I'm too dry."

"I know," he whispered back. He kissed her, then rolled off of her onto his back. He was understanding. He could feel she was in pain, so he stopped as soon as she said she was too dry. He loved her and did not want to hurt her.

The two of them lay on their backs next to each other, still filled with desire. After a few moments, David gently whispered a request he expected Sarah to decline because he believed she was not the type to do something like that, but his desire to bond with her sexually was so strong, he needed something. So he shyly whispered: "Will you give me head?" Sarah responded with a passionate whisper: "Yes! But let me kiss you, first." She then rolled on top of him and began a long passionate, full tongue kiss. She thought he was so sweet. She could hear the tentativeness in his question and knew he expected her to say no. But she loved him. She wanted to please him. She hated the thought of leaving him hard and unsatisfied. His idea was a good one. She would kiss him and love him with her mouth until he came.

She was on top of him now, kissing his mouth passionately. She was surprised at how passionately David received and returned her kisses. He was the one prolonging the kiss. Sarah had thought that a man requesting a blowjob would've been in a hurry to feel her lips around his erection. But instead, David was savoring her passionate kiss, and making it last longer. This made her love David so much more. She gave him a little more of that kiss, but she wasn't going to make him wait much longer for what he requested. She slowly pulled her mouth away from David's lips and quickly kissed his neck breaking free from the kiss but not the intimate bond it created. She pressed her lips to his neck and gave him a long kiss there. His body responded with pleasure. He pressed into her kiss, "mmmm," he moaned. She then kissed across his chest, and began a downward trail of kisses. His head relaxed backwards as he exhaled a whisper of pleasure: "Ah."

Sarah's trail of kisses reached his stomach now. She lifted her head and stared at his erection. She loved his penis. It was so perfect. She appreciated how it fit inside her so perfectly, and gave her so much pleasure. She stared adoringly at his perfect penis, wanting to return the pleasure it gave her. Then she wrapped her lips around the tip and sucked twice. She then opened her mouth and licked with a delicate upward gesture, starting just an inch below the tip. She then swirled her tongue around the tip. Wrapping her lips around him, she began her descent, sucking on the way down until her lips reached the bottom of his shaft and his entire cock was completely immersed in her mouth. David's sounds of pleasure grew louder now, though still just a whispered: "Ah, ah..."

She loved the feel of his dick in her mouth, pressing against the walls of her mouth and her tongue. It reminded her of how amazing his dick felt inside her. This made her vagina crave the feel of his cock. She used that desire to deliver David all her passion as she sucked and bobbed his beautiful cock in a steady rhythm now. The more she sucked on him, the more her vagina ached for the feel of his cock. It was starting to make her just a little wet, but still not quite enough moisture to ease the rawness.

As Sarah's gentle but firm rhythm continued, David's pleasure was heightening. His whispered moans and sighs of pleasure were continuous. Sarah had never heard him express so much pleasure, so she kept going. Then, in the middle of a moan, David whispered seductively, pleading: "Please fuck me." Sarah responded immediately. She lifted her head, sliding her body upwards, kissing him along the way; pressing her breasts against him until she was high enough to slide her vagina over his cock. Then she rocked him. She held him in a close embrace as she rocked him hard hoping to make him come fast. Her vagina was still sore but moist enough to make the pain more bearable. She imagined that once he came, the feel of his cum would sooth her soreness. So she rocked him and fucked him hard, trying to make him come. David could feel in the way she rocked him, with her tight vagina firmly grasping his cock, moving up and down with determination, that she did this for him. She was demanding his orgasm. She was not seeking her own.

So, for the first time in his life, David just relaxed and indulged in the pleasure of sex only for himself, without holding back for the woman to orgasm first. Then he burst with his own orgasm, his cum filling her up inside. The dryness in her vagina made the burst of his cum feel more sensuous. She reveled in the feeling of receiving it. It was a soothing cream lining the walls of her vagina, instantly relieving all the pain and rawness she had previously felt. Sarah exhaled a loud: "Aaaaaahhh" as she squeezed him tight during his orgasm. When he finished coming, she kissed him and rolled over onto the bed, still wrapping one arm and one leg around him. She exhaled breathlessly and whispered in his ear: "That was amazing! That was sooo amazing." David looked at her with surprise. Did she orgasm? He didn't feel her body's typical gyrations during an orgasm.

Sarah was so filled with satisfaction that she couldn't tell if she had orgasmed with David, or if it was the feel of his orgasm that satiated her desire. During the act, she had not felt her own body physically orgasm. But after holding him so tight during his orgasm and relishing in the feeling of receiving his cum, Sarah felt the afterglow she usually feels after she has an orgasm. David and Sarah's bond was so strong physically, sexually, spiritually, and emotionally, that Sarah had felt the pleasure of David's orgasm.

On her way to work later that morning, Sarah noticed every wedding dress shop along the way. She had never noticed these shops before. This made her smile. "I finally found the man that I am most definitely going to marry," she thought.

Sarah got to work a little late that day. She was never late, but she didn't care today. The precious moment she shared with David this morning was so perfect, she wouldn't change it for the world. Had she really felt his orgasm instead of her own? That was so amazing. Their bond was something she never dreamed of. She never imagined that two people could be so close. For the first time in her life, she was annoyed to be at work. It now felt like her work prevented her from spending more time with David. The only thing she wanted anymore was to spend all her time with David.

As she walked towards her office, she was intercepted by an experienced Detective on the White Collar Crime Team. Detective Jones grabbed her by the arm and said:

"Hey, you need to come with me, now."

"But I have to ..."

"No, this is important. The White Collar Crime Team is meeting in 10 minutes, and you're the head of that team, so we need you there. I can't let the guys run with this without the direction of the District Attorney's Office. They're all excited that the suspect is some Hollywood big shot. They all want to be the first to arrest the big fish."

"Arrest? You know no arrests are made in white collar crime cases until I've reviewed the evidence and determined there's sufficient probably cause. Usually I require a grand jury indictment first."

"I know. That's why you need to be there."

Sarah hurried off with the Detective. She found a group of less experienced officers in the room, acting like rowdy teenagers. She was glad to have Detective Jones there. He was the only detective left on the team with any real experience. Two retirements this year lost her two out of three of her best detectives. She only had one good one now plus a group of "children" (as she saw them) who would rather be handling sexier crimes like robberies or drug deals, not this bookkeeping crap that none of them had the patience for. They liked physical evidence: guns, drugs, pictures of bloody crime scenes. They didn't like documents and bank statements. The young ones always viewed being stuck on the White Collar Crime Team as punishment, an initiation of sorts. Sarah cursed the department for not carefully selecting only officers who actually demonstrated some proficiency in reading, writing and accounting. But the Chief had told her once: "that's what expert witnesses are for." He explained that all he needed was an officer with a badge and a gun who could collect evidence and make arrests. He had also explained to Sarah: "Besides, they hone their investigation skills serving on your team. You make them think. You prepare their minds to become great murder case detectives. I make every one of my rookies serve on your team at some point in their career or another." She knew the Chief had given her a huge compliment that day, but she still hated him for it.

Sarah walked over to a near-empty coffee pot and poured the last bit of cheap, stale coffee into her cup as she listened to the "boys" plot how they would best like to make the arrest.

"Should we do it during one of his major parties in his great big Hollywood mansion?"

"No stupid! You don't want hundreds of drunks surrounding you when you're making an arrest. You know how dangerous that can be."

"Well, I just thought --"

"No, you didn't think at all."

Sarah smiled with her back still turned to the officers. She was glad Detective Jones was there to explain to them that this was not a game. Even white-collar criminals could be dangerous.

Sarah didn't follow celebrity news and had no idea who was getting these officers in such a tizzy. She didn't even think to ask who it was. She walked over to the table where the officers sat and asked:

"What do you got?"

Officer Smart began: "A written confession!"

"What do you mean, 'a written confession?' These guys aren't usually that stupid."

"It's right here. A "how to" book. It was found just sitting on his dining room table. Well, it's not really a book. But it's a printed document that explains in detail, exactly how he plans to defraud a group of people out of millions of dollars. He has their names listed, the amount of money they would invest, the bank account it would be deposited into, and the fake movie they were supposed to be investing in. Then, suddenly the money in their accounts is all gone. It's moved into an offshore account. No money, no movie. The money's all his to enjoy."

Sarah flipped through the pages, and it was just as the officer had described. Names, Account Numbers, Investment Amounts and specific instructions on how to get victims to open accounts in their own names, then wire the money to off-shore accounts where money could easily be moved and distributed without being traced by the FBI, thereby hiding the identity of the true recipient.

It included a section called: 'The Story,' which apparently described the story he would tell investors to convince them to go through the steps of opening an account in their own name into which all funds would be deposited, then wiring all funds to a specified off-shore account the same day the deposit was made. He would tell them the investment was for a movie being made in a foreign country. It was easier for them to wire the funds themselves directly into the off-shore investment account, as he would be away for several weeks getting things organized abroad for movie production, and therefore could not meet with them to pick up a check. He would tell them not to worry, as the offshore account would be in the name of an entity that bore the same name of the movie's title.

It was a brilliant plan. It kept his hands off the financial transactions and his identity hidden. But in the same way that the "written confession" so neatly presented all the evidence reflecting his intent to defraud, the identity of the victims, the account numbers and amounts, etc., it also contained a very questionable ending. The last line of the "written confession" stated: "But the truth is, there is no movie! The money is all mine!" That was very strange. It almost sounded planted. As if someone was trying to manufacture a picture of guilt. The rest of the document made sense. To keep track of his plan, a criminal might plot it out and write it down. One that involved telling different stories to different people, may need to be written and memorized. A record of who would invest and how much, was helpful if he ever needed to discuss the fake investment with the investor and come up with a later excuse for why the movie flopped, or how disaster struck and it couldn't be finished. It made sense for the suspect to make notes so he could remember what to say to who. However, it did not make sense for him to leave written evidence of the fact that the movie was not real. This haunted Sarah. Was this or wasn't this a real confession?

Sarah then asked Officer Smart: "Did you seize the computer this 'written confession' was typed on?"

There was silence.

She looked around the room at each of the officers. None of them spoke. This was usually a sign that the cops had fucked up. Sarah was immediately angry.

Waiving the written confession, Sarah demanded: "Which one of you seized this evidence?!"

Officer Smart and Officer Derek indicated it was them.

"How did you get this evidence?"

Officer Smart answered: "Search Warrant."

"How did you get a search warrant?"

"One of the victims came forward. He said that when he was visiting the suspect in his Hollywood home, he saw the 'written confession' sitting on the dining room table. He said he flipped through it while the suspect was in the bathroom, out of curiosity to see who invested in what. Then he saw the last line: 'But the truth is, there is no movie! The money is all mine!' That's when he called us and we got the search warrant."

"I assume the search warrant included authority to seize any electronic data, computers and any electronic devices..."

Officer Smart looked down and mumbled: "Yes."

"Then where the hell is it!"

"Why would we need that? We had the written confession sitting on his dining room table, in his house! In plain sight! I probably didn't even need a search warrant to get that!"

"What the fuck did you say!? You didn't need a search warrant to get that!? Then how the fuck would you have authority to enter his home and take something!!!!"

Sarah was enraged. These officers were far stupider then she thought before she had walked in. They were in a hurry to arrest some Hollywood big shot who was sure to attract media attention, who was sure to hire the best lawyers, and these dumb fuckers wanted to make an arrest without first having gathered all the evidence. A poor investigation would make the District Attorney's Office look like a laughing stock.

"Describe to me now. Everything you did in execution of the search warrant. Give me the step by step details."

"Well, we knocked on the door and a butler answered. We asked if the suspect was home and he let us in and asked us to wait a few minutes because he thought he should be getting home any time now. We asked if we could be seated at the dining room table because that is where the witness had said the 'written confession' was when he saw it. And I'll be damned if it wasn't sitting right there when the butler sat us down. The butler left so we flipped through it to see if it fit the description of what the witness had described. And it did! Exactly! Then we saw the bottom line where he's fucking bragging to himself: 'But the truth is, there is no movie! The money is all mine!' We had a solid written confession and a witness on the list of investors who said he invested money. That was all we needed. So we took the 'written confession.' I rolled it up around my billy club and placed it back into my utility belt so the butler wouldn't notice we had taken something. Then we told him we had an emergency call and that we would be in touch with his boss if we still needed to speak to him later. The butler had no idea we were there for the search warrant. The confession was in plain sight. We have an eyewitness. So what else do we need?"

"What else do you fucking need?! How about evidence that your witness didn't plant the 'written confession'! How about evidence of who actually authored the fucking thing! How about the goddamn computers in his home that you had authority to seize while you were there! How about bank records to show the money was in fact invested! To show where the fuck it went! To show who is in control of it! How about evidence that what you've picked up, isn't itself just a movie script! How about evidence that the movies identified aren't real movies!!!!"

"But the suspect confesses right here that they are not real movies!"

"I have to prove that!"

"But he says it!"

Through gritted teeth, Sarah repeated herself, slowly, as if holding back a major explosion: "I said, I have to fucking prove that. A confession alone is not enough. I need independent evidence corroborating the confession!" The word "confession" burst out of her, with the loud explosion she'd been holding back through her gritted teeth.

"But the witness --"

"Do you want to try this case!? Do you want to try this fucking case!? Are you an attorney?! Can you stand in front of a jury and prove this case beyond a reasonable doubt!?"

"No."

"Then get me my fucking evidence!"

Sarah was standing now. Pointing angrily in the officer's face. Although she was wearing a dress and high heels, the officers did not see a woman standing there. They saw an angry D.A. And they were going to follow her instructions because they didn't want to be described as officers who performed sloppy investigations.

There was silence in the room, now. Sarah sat down and grabbed the "written confession." She flipped through the pages angrily. She was looking for something more. Looking for additional leads she would send the officers to pursue. Sarah studied the "written confession" as they had been calling it. A different crime would be charged for each victim listed. She looked at the list of investors and noticed that each name had the name of a different movie title, and therefore listed a different offshore account into which the investment would be wired. This would make it easier to argue for consecutive sentencing for each victim. This meant that during the sentencing hearing, which would take place after trial, the defense could not argue that this was one scheme requiring all sentences on all charges to be served during the same time period. If that were the case, it would have allowed 25 different 7 year sentences to equal a total of only 7 years because the defendant would serve them all at the same time. However, the different movie titles and different accounts of investment created a situation where Sarah could argue that each movie was a different scheme to defraud a different person; therefore, a 7-year sentence for the crime relating to one victim had to be served first, before the 7-year sentence for the next victim could begin to run. This would make two 7-year sentences equal 14 years. There were enough different victims and different movie names on the list, that stacking the sentences in this way would result in a long enough sentence to send the suspect away for life, whatever his age.

Sarah then asked the officer: "Whose your suspect?"

The officer handed her a photograph downloaded from the suspect's Facebook page.

Sarah looked at it and almost puked. The first thing that struck her were his big blue eyes. She stared into them and felt that overwhelming connection that drew her in but made her stomach turn even more violently. The man in the picture was David. Her beloved David. The man who rescued her from rape. The man she gave her virginity to. The man she loved so much she couldn't bear to be away from him. The suspect was David! She couldn't believe it. This couldn't be true. It couldn't be happening. The suspect couldn't be David! David didn't even have a house in Hollywood. He lived in Malibu. Or was there a huge part of David's life that he'd been hiding from her? What else was he hiding? Was he really a criminal? There had to be some explanation for this. The suspect could not be David!

"Sarah? Are you ok? You look like you're going to be sick," Detective Jones said.

Sarah lied: "I think I ate bad sushi last night." She needed a cover. She couldn't let anyone know about her connection to David. She'd be kicked off the case. She needed to stay involved. She needed to know if he was guilty or innocent. She needed to know for certain, for herself. She couldn't allow some other Deputy D.A. to handle the case. She couldn't take the jury's word for it. What if he was guilty but they acquitted? Worse! What if he was innocent but they convicted?! He could go away for life! An innocent man, her beloved David, incarcerated for life! Sarah was going to be sick.

Sarah excused herself: "I think that sushi wants to come up and revisit, excuse me guys!" She ran to the ladies room and vomited. After washing her mouth and face with cold water, she leaned against the wall next to the sink and slid down it. She was too weak to stand. She sat on the floor, holding her knees to her chest and she just stared, thoughtlessly for several minutes. She needed to regroup. A person could be sick from sushi for three days. That would be her excuse. Taking a deep breath and gathering as much strength as she could, Sarah walked back into the room the officers were gathered in and said:

"Nothing happens until you've retrieved the evidence I've instructed you to retrieve. If I determine it is sufficient, first we interview the suspect before an arrest. An arrest will trigger the hiring of lawyers and we may never get his initial un-edited statement that will otherwise be carefully crafted by counsel before he speaks to us. And, there will NOT be an arrest before there is an indictment. I'm going home now. The last time I was sick off sushi, it lasted three days. This case can wait three days." She then left without waiting for the officers to respond. She had used all her strength to muster up those words. She couldn't face the world now, the way she was feeling. She hurried to her car and drove straight home to her little apartment in Santa Monica.

When Sarah got home, she drew all her drapes shut, turned out the lights and laid on her bed. She genuinely did feel sick. She would give herself one day to be sick. But the next two days she had to sit and think about everything. She had to develop a strategy for figuring things out. But right now, she was in no state to think clearly. She fell asleep hard. She didn't wake until it was dark outside. She had turned her phone off and therefore missed all of David's calls.

Sarah woke to the sound of the roar of a Lamborghini's engine outside her window. She knew instantly it was David. She started to feel panic well up insider her. Her feelings confused her. She didn't know if she loved him or hated him. Actually, she knew. She knew she loved him deeply. And, that scared her to death. Could she still love him this deeply if he was guilty? She tried to imagine him guilty, but it didn't shake the feeling inside her that was so deep it reached her soul: She loved him. That was a fact she could never get away from. David was at her door now, knocking frantically. "Sarah? Sarah, are you in there? Sarah, please be home, please be ok. I've been calling but you haven't answered."

Sarah's heart melted. Poor David. He has no idea he is a suspect. He is worried about her well-being. She walked over to her front door and stopped. She couldn't let him in. They couldn't speak. It would be inappropriate. It would ruin her own personal investigation, and her opportunity to control the official investigation. It could jeopardize him as well. If it appeared he was romantically involved with a Deputy D.A., it would be harder to prove he was truly innocent and not simply a guilty man under her protection.

Sarah touched the door that separated them. She could feel his presence on the other side. She could hear his sweet, loving voice of concern. It destroyed her. She leaned against the door and slipped to the ground. Tears started rolling down her face. She tried not to sob so that he wouldn't hear her. The pain was unbearable. She wanted to be with him so bad. She wanted to know if he was guilty or innocent. She wanted to see his beautiful blue eyes in person, not in a picture as a suspect. She wanted to look into his eyes and ask all her questions. His eyes would tell her if he was being truthful or deceitful. She could get the answers she wanted if she would just open the door and look into his eyes.

She could still hear his voice. "Sarah! Sarah, are you in there!" She could feel his fear that something terrible had happened to her. She never avoided his calls. He could always reach her if she was not in court, and court never lasted after 5:00 p.m. It was 10:00 p.m. now and she hadn't been answering his calls. Sarah sat on the floor with her knees drawn up to her chest. She sat curled up with her arms around her knees, leaning against the door, hear heart and soul reaching towards his, yearning to be closer to him. She held in her sobs as the pain in her heart continued to grow. She put one hand over her mouth and let out a silent cry into her hand. Her chest was constricting and she was losing her breath trying to hold in the sound. She wanted to shout out his name, but she couldn't talk to him now. It would ruin everything. Also, she had this debilitating fear that he might be guilty. She didn't want to be charmed by a con artist. It could destroy her career. Sarah sat there, crying silently until David gave up. She listened to the roar of his Lamborghini drive off, then she let out a whaling cry, as she sobbed out loud, finally able to release her pain with desperate sobs. She grabbed onto the door handle to help herself up. She walked over to the bedroom where she collapsed onto the bed and continued to cry until she fell asleep.

David drove home distraught. He couldn't understand why he couldn't reach Sarah. This never happened. They both had enough respect for each other to always answer each other's calls. Something had to be wrong. David could feel that something was very wrong. He didn't know what to do though. You can't call in a missing person's report just because your girlfriend didn't return your calls. The frustration was killing him. The feelings of helplessness were overwhelming. His greatest fear was that she was in trouble again, like the day he found her. He was so afraid that she was in danger and he couldn't protect her. He tried to think. What could he do? How could he find her? He tried to clear his mind and feel for his instincts. Maybe he would get some type of sign. He drove to his Malibu mansion and walked to his upstairs balcony. It was dark and the wind carried a chill, but he needed the fresh air and an unobstructed sound of the ocean. He breathed in the ocean breeze with a deep breath. He sat in his favorite chair on the balcony and waited for some feeling or thought to tell him where to go find Sarah. But he could only picture her at her apartment. He was already there. She didn't answer. He needed to talk to someone. So he called Frank.

"Just relax," Frank said. "It's only been a few hours."

"But she never does this. Something is wrong. I can tell something is wrong."

"Listen, this happens at some point in every relationship, one of the parties gets lazy and more time passes between calls."

"No! Not Sarah and I! We're not even close to that point in our relationship! We'll probably never get close to that point." David thought of the amazing sex marathon they had the night before. He thought of the amazing blowjob she'd given him this morning. He thought of how she orgasmed with him and held him sweetly, telling him how amazing it was. No. It was impossible. Sarah was not just being too lazy to return his calls.

"Frank. Sarah is in trouble. I can feel it."

"You can feel it? What are you a woman now, with sixth senses and everything?"

"Shut the fuck up, you asshole!" David didn't only hang up on Frank, he threw his phone across the balcony and heard it shatter. He was so angry. He would never be able to explain to anyone how he knew, deep inside, that something terrible was happening.

CHAPTER 20

Officer Smart needed reaffirmation that he was not incompetent. So he decided to ask another Deputy D.A. his opinion of the case. Sarah had a reputation for being tough, and demanding an airtight case, but not all cases could be airtight. He was hoping to find someone in the D.A.'s Office who agreed that he had sufficient evidence to proceed to grand jury and make an arrest. He did not intend to ignore Sarah's demands for additional evidence. He just wanted someone to tell him they agreed with him.

Officer Smart asked Deputy D.A. Hagard for an audience. He was the only one who would agree to meet with him to discuss one of Sarah's cases. Hagard had his own issues with Sarah. He resented her. He resented the fact that she was so revered by all, even defense attorneys who always called her one of their "most worthy opponents." She was appointed as the head of various crime teams. She was assigned the most high profile cases. There was always a buzz about how she won cases people thought couldn't be won. She was complimented by their boss, the District Attorney himself, for her ability to direct officers in continuing to investigate crimes until an airtight case could be created. It made him sick. She was always in the limelight.

They had been classmates in law school. They had started working at the D.A.'s Office on the same day six years ago. But she got all the credit and he was ignored. He thought it was unfair. He thought she was just given more opportunities than him. He felt he was stuck in the misdemeanor division and was not given the same opportunities she was given. The reality was, her talent was recognized immediately and so her responsibilities grew, and as her responsibilities grew, so did her glory. But Hagard could not admit this to himself. He insisted he was denied the opportunity to show everyone what he's got. So when Officer Smart approached him, Deputy D.A. Hagard was happy to meet. Hagard wanted an opportunity to one-up Sarah, and this sounded like it was his chance.

After Officer Smart explained everything to Hagard, Hagard thought to himself that Officer Smart had brought him the perfect opportunity. He would take this case to grand jury while Sarah was out sick. It would become his case. He would show everyone that he could try a case that Sarah was too scared to charge because she thought a written confession and a witness wasn't enough evidence. And if he could convict a Hollywood big shot, oh man! He'd really be in the limelight then! He'd be the stud Deputy D.A. And she'd be a coward. Hagard told Officer Smart to bring the witness in to testify at grand jury the next day.

The next day, while Sarah was home sick thinking the officers were following her instructions, Hagard presented the case to the grand jury. Detective Jones was walking past the grand jury room when he saw the witness standing in the hall waiting for his case to be called. Detective Jones asked him what he was doing there.

"Officer Smart said I had to be here."

"Why?"

"To testify"

"About what?"

"The fraud case for that asshole who stole my money for a fake movie!"

Detective Jones walked away and immediately called Sarah. Sarah was still in bed and reached for her phone:

"What? You know I'm sick."

"Did you give the instruction to send the new fraud case we met about yesterday to grand jury?"

"No. Why?"

"Well, someone's presenting it today."

"What!"

"I saw the witness in front of the grand jury room. He said he's here to testify."

Sarah hung up the phone and threw on her clothes. She rushed to the D.A.'s Office as quickly as she could. On her drive in, she called Detective Jones to get an update on the investigation. He informed her that none of the other victims were returning calls. He thought their reluctance had to do with the fact that they were all convicted criminals. There was a strange theme. All the men were convicted drug dealers. All the women were convicted prostitutes. The witness who had come forward was a drug dealer out on parole.

Sarah got to the D.A.'s Office in time to see Hagard standing with the case file in his hand, bragging to the staff: "Guess who I just indicted." Sarah ripped the file out of his hands and saw David's name on it. She marched towards the largest office at the end of the hall, which was occupied by the District Attorney himself. Hagard ran after her: "Hey! What do you think you're doing?!" She did not acknowledge him.

The District Attorney was sitting at his desk. Sarah sat in a chair across from him and said, "We need to talk." Hagard was right behind her. When he entered the room, Sarah decided to put Hagard on trial.

With the level of poise and eloquence she ordinarily reserves for her presentations to judges and juries, Sarah began:

"I would like to know, why Mr. Hagard, who is in the misdemeanor department, has usurped my authority as the head of the White Collar Crime Team and presented a case to grand jury when I specifically instructed the officers on my team to gather more evidence before the case could be presented to grand jury?"

The DA looked at Hagard with a scowl. "Is this true?"

"What difference does it make? I got the indictment. Of course we have sufficient evidence. We have a confession and a witness. Doesn't the indictment prove we have sufficient evidence?"

Sarah answered Hagard's stupid question, without sacrificing her poise. She directed her words to the DA:

"If Mr. Hagard had any experience with felony cases, he would understand that an indictment is much easier to obtain than a conviction. The grand jury only hears one side of the story. They are asked only if probable cause exists to charge a crime. The trial jury will hear the defendant's side of the story and must determine guilt beyond a reasonable doubt. Now, we have lost our opportunity to obtain the defendant's statement, and prepare our response to his side of the story before trial, because he will hire a lawyer who will instruct him not to speak to us. We have the added problem that we cannot prove who wrote the alleged written confession because the officers did not seize any computers when they were in his home with a search warrant in hand. The "confession" has its own internal credibility problems that any high-dollar lawyer in town will blow out of the water. The witness is a twice-over convicted drug dealer who is out on parole. No other alleged victims have returned officers' calls. If they were real and they did in fact have a substantial amount of money stolen from them, we would expect them to return calls immediately wondering how to get their money back. Furthermore, they too are all convicted criminals."

Hagard tried to stand his ground: "She sounds like a defense lawyer!"

The DA responded: "That's why she wins cases. Now get the hell out of my office and don't ever pull a stunt like this again!"

After Hagard left, the DA turned to Sarah: "Do you think I should fire him?"

Sarah thought he certainly should be fired for deviating so substantially from the hierarchy of the D.A.'s Office, which was designed to maintain the integrity of the D.A.'s Office. But she was softhearted and just couldn't get herself to say the words. So instead, she said, "That's not my call to make."

The DA appreciated Sarah's good character. Anyone else would have perceived this as a personal attack and would have jumped at the opportunity to fire an ambitious usurper, especially one whose stupidity jeopardized a high profile case. He shared Sarah's unspoken thoughts about how highly unacceptable the behavior was and decided he would fire Hagard. But he didn't need to burden Sarah with his decision. After all, she was right. It was not her call to make.

Sarah walked to her desk and began making phone calls. She needed to make arrangements for David's arraignment. She would not allow the case to be processed as usual and sent out for an arrest warrant to be issued. If David was going to be incarcerated, it had to be after his arraignment where the Court would decide whether to jail or release him pending trial. Usually a man with substantial assets would be considered a high flight risk and might be incarcerated pending trial. Sarah wanted this file handled with care. So she called the Court's clerk herself (a task normally left for staff), and asked them to give her an arraignment date for the new case. She then called the entertainment lawyer whose name she heard David mention often as the attorney who represented him in his entertainment business transactions.

"I am calling from the District Attorney's Office to extend a courtesy to you and one of your clients. He has been indicted and his arraignment is set for next Tuesday at 9:00 a.m. We will not issue an arrest warrant if he appears at his arraignment. His physical presence is required. You may not appear on his behalf. If he fails to appear at his arraignment, an arrest warrant will be issued."

After answering all the lawyer's questions, Sarah hung up the phone. She had not given the attorney her name. She merely identified herself as "an attorney" from the D.A.'s Office. She could not bear the thought of David finding out about his indictment and hearing at the same time that it was his own girlfriend who made the call. Oh God! David! Sarah thought of him now and she felt ill again. Her beautiful blue-eyed man had been indicted and she herself was not even sure he was guilty. As she explained the problems with the case to the DA, she grew more convinced that he was innocent. She hated that piece of shit Haggard for screwing things up before she could complete a proper investigation. She told herself to keep her head. She had to stay focused. Now, it was more important than ever to stay focused and insure David was not wrongfully convicted (if in fact he was innocent).

Sarah knew that once a case had been through grand jury, and an indictment issued, it was very difficult to undo what had been done. Sometimes there was no way out other than to let the case go to trial and see what the jury would do. But juries had convicted innocent people before. The system was not guaranteed to deliver the correct result.

CHAPTER 21

When David entered the courtroom, he saw Sarah, and froze. She was standing at counsel table with her back to the audience. But it was unmistakably her. David knew the curve of her body. He knew it so well, he could see it through that conservative business suit she wore. He wouldn't miss those curves anywhere. He had every inch of them memorized. Her long black hair, which he had witnessed on so many occasions dangling down her bare skin, was now wound up in a tight bun. But he could still see, that was his beloved Sarah. The woman he loved. The woman who changed him the moment he first saw her. Even before he knew her name, she had changed him. He had wanted to make her his wife. He had wanted to love her, cherish her and protect her.

Ironically, now it seemed he was the one who needed protection from her. The thought scared him so badly it immobilized him. David stood there staring at Sarah's back, frozen with fear. The woman he loved had the power, the means, and the opportunity to destroy him. He couldn't breathe.

David's attorney saw the look on David's face and assumed it was the large jail deputy standing next to Sarah that put so much fear in David's face. He immediately stood in front of David so as to block his view of the jailor, which luckily, also blocked his view of Sarah. He needed his client focused. He needed him to look relaxed but not cocky, just like they had practiced. Dan Goldstein needed his client to look innocent. David's attorney began to speak:

"Don't worry David, I'm not going to let that big guy take you away. I won't let the judge require more bail than what you've told me you can post today. We've talked about this. Just relax and trust me to do my job. All I need you to do is relax. Don't look in that direction. Think of something else."

David responded to his attorney's words by looking down at the floor.

"No. Don't look down. That looks like guilt. Look at me. Look at me for a minute."

As David lifted his face to meet his attorney's eyes, the attorney began to speak. "You are an innocent man. It is impossible for you to be guilty. You don't ask for investments. Other people ask you to invest. You are an innocent man. I know you are innocent and it's going to be very easy for me to prove that. We just have to get through this procedure of ensuring your release pending trial. The rest is a breeze. Stay with me David."

David's focus on his lawyer helped him relax a little. He took a deep breath, and the breath lifted his strength. He stood taller now. His previously slumped shoulders were now pulled back in confidence, his was chin up and a relaxed look of innocence returned to his face. There was still a glint of fear in his eyes, but that was good. An innocent man, unfamiliar with the criminal justice system, should be afraid of this foreign atmosphere. At least the look of anger and contempt were gone now. That was good.

David heard his name in the title of the next case that was called. His lawyer stood between him and the opposite counsel table, where Sarah was standing. David made sure not to look in that direction as he walked towards the defense side of counsel table with his lawyer. David stared straight ahead at the judge, looking the judge in the eye, as if to say, "I have nothing to hide. I am innocent." The judge began to read the charges. David did not recognize any of the alleged victims names. He wondered how it was possible to charge a man with a crime against people he had never heard of. Maybe one of the female names sounded vaguely familiar, but not really. David swallowed hard and tried not to pass out when the Court asked him:

"Do you understand that the maximum penalty could add up to more than 100 years in prison?"

David looked the judge in the eye and said: "Yes, I understand."

"How do you plead to the charges?"

"Not Guilty."

"I will turn now to the prosecution, what is your recommendation with respect to bail and release?"

The sound of Sarah's voice startled David. His heart began to beat rapidly as she spoke. He wondered if she would ask that he be held in jail without bail. Then he heard Sarah say:

"Your Honor, The Defendant has no criminal history, whatsoever, not even an arrest. It appears that this is his first brush with the law. I recommend that the Defendant be released on his own recognizance."

The judge was surprised by her recommendation. His eyebrows shot up as he commented: "This isn't like you Ms. Cartwright."

"The investigation is ongoing, Your Honor." Sarah chose her words carefully. She wanted to alert the judge to the fact that she had doubts as to the man's guilt, but she could not say that directly. She needed to use code language to make the Court understand that it was her belief that justice required the Court to go very light on him, at this juncture.

The judge responded, a little perplexed: "Well, it isn't like you to indict before you've completed your investigation, either."

Sarah Answered: "I wasn't the attorney handling grand jury your honor. It was handled by another attorney in my office while I was out sick."

A look that said "I got it, now" crossed the judge's face, and Sarah knew her message was delivered.

The criminal defense lawyer couldn't believe his ears! Sarah was practically telling the judge she doubted the case! Practically admitting that they didn't have enough evidence to proceed! This was a gift from heaven! He was taking it!

"Your honor, Ms. Cartwright is a highly respected prosecutor who ordinarily asks for very high bail and very strict release conditions. I think when she tells you the Defendant should be released on his own recognizance, you can trust her instincts. It isn't often I say this, but I strongly urge the Court to follow the prosecutor's recommendation."

This made the judge crack a smile. It was indeed a little funny to hear a defense lawyer say he agreed with a prosecutor. The judge then said: "I will take your recommendation, Ms. Cartwright. I am releasing the Defendant without bail. However, I will require him to restrict his movements to the boundaries of Los Angeles County. He must wear a detection device that will alert the Sheriff's Office if he leaves that boundary."

David's attorney patted him on the back, happily. David sighed with relief. He didn't have to go to jail, not yet, at least. He was still being treated like a criminal, but at least he was not going to be incarcerated. His lawyer turned to him and said: "Let's go get a drink."

Sarah knew the move she just made was a very dangerous one. Normally in a case such as this, she would argue that there was not a bail amount high enough to deter a man with such assets from fleeing justice after posting bail. Normally, she would have asked the court to hold the

Defendant in jail pending trial, without bail. If anyone had seen her with David previously, and news traveled back to the D.A.'s Office, it would appear that she had re-asserted herself into the case in order to favor her boyfriend and intentionally sabotage the case for his benefit. By now she knew that Haggard had been fired, and that made the whole picture look even worse. If the media caught wind of how heavily David donated to police officer charities, it would become even uglier. If her relationship with David were ever discovered, it would end her career. Not only would she get fired from the D.A.'s Office, she would never work as an attorney again. She would be seen as someone who put her personal interest ahead of her duties as an attorney, when ethics required attorneys to step away from cases in which they had personal conflicts. And this was indisputably, a personal conflict. But Sarah's motives were not to destroy the case. Her motive was to serve justice. She needed to use the resources of the D.A.'s Office to prove to herself what David really was - guilty or innocent. If someone else had to actually be the attorney handling the trial, so be it. But she had to lead the investigation. The investigation was not yet complete. And she had to be the one to finish it. She could only do that by maintaining control of the case, and hiding her relationship with David.

At drinks, David's lawyer was telling him he couldn't believe how lucky he'd gotten. He'd never seen Sarah Cartwright do that. Usually she was a shark. She was one of the meanest (and the best) Deputy D.A.'s in the D.A.'s Office. And judges always followed her recommendations, both at sentencing hearings and at arraignments. He couldn't believe this had happened today! He explained, excitedly: "This is a good sign, it's a very good sign! It means she doesn't believe in the case! Someone charged the case without her knowledge. This is good David! This is very good! I will be calling her first thing in the morning. I will see if I can convince her to dismiss the case."

David wasn't smiling. He was still shaken up by the whole experience. He wasn't sure his lawyer's assessment of the position of the D.A.'s Office's was correct. He asked his lawyer: "Does it make a difference that she's my girlfriend?"

The attorney spit out his beverage, almost choking on it. "What!?"

On his drive home to his sanctuary in Malibu, David kept re-living the day's events. Sarah in the courtroom prosecuting him, the judge looking surprised at her recommendation, his lawyer telling him what a good sign it was that she recommended release, then spitting out his drink when David asked if it made a difference that she was his girlfriend. The attorney had not indicated one way or the other. He just looked completely abashed and actually seemed to no longer be sure of his earlier assessment. All he said was: "I'll be investigating all the circumstances and will keep you informed."

David remembered how Sarah disappeared on him and refused to return any of his calls the day before his entertainment lawyer called him to give him the news of the indictment and to recommend Dan Goldstein. She had told him that Dan was a first-rate criminal defense attorney who could win cases on his reputation alone. She specifically instructed him not to discuss the case with anyone, not his girlfriend, not his mother, not his best friend.

"Girlfriend." That word popped out at him the most. It stung his ears like venom. *"Girlfriend,"* David had thought in that moment, "where *is* my girlfriend?" Of course, David immediately knew that the indictment was the reason she had disappeared on him like that. And that thought scared him. It scared him. It angered him. And it disgusted him. How could she? How could she abandon him at a time like this? If she loved him, why wouldn't she step in and protect him? Why wouldn't she use her influence to assist? Why hadn't she reached out to his defense lawyer to help defend him? And why? Why the hell would she let him find out this way, instead of telling him herself? All these questions made David

sick to his stomach. He didn't know Sarah anymore. He felt like a fool for ever having loved her as he did.

As David drove past the gated entrance to his Malibu mansion, his feelings of anger and confusion turned into feelings of sadness and loss. This was the very first place he brought Sarah when he saved her from rape. This was the place he protected her and gave her back her strength. This was the place they fell in love and instantly became an inseparable couple. It was hard to drive up this driveway without thinking about those moments.

David was exhausted from the stress of the past week, all building until the arraignment he had today, the fear of not knowing if he'd be going to jail, followed by the trauma of being marked like an animal with a tracking device, and the devastation of seeing the woman he loves prosecuting him for a long list of crimes that could put him away for life. It was all too much to bear. He could feel himself physically becoming weaker.

As David stepped inside his home, he looked around. It felt different now. Somehow, the place didn't feel right. Then he realized what was so wrong. Sarah. The place was missing Sarah. It didn't feel the same without her anymore. He then realized he had lost more than his girlfriend today. He also lost his sanctuary. This was no longer David's sanctuary. It was Sarah's. She had told him once that her favorite place in the whole world was a place he created in his backyard, a place they called the Garden of Eden. This place belonged to Sarah now. Just as Sarah had given David her precious virginity in his Garden of Eden, David had given Sarah, his entire sanctuary.

It hurt too much to stand in this place without her. The pain David felt in his heart and soul was overwhelming. It was debilitating. He needed to sit down. He couldn't walk any further into the house. But he also didn't have the physical strength to drive away. He felt like he was going to collapse. David put his hand over his racing heart as he stumbled, and landed on the nearest couch. He reached for his phone in his pocket, turned it off and slid it away from him across the floor. He laid his head down in the cushions and took a long deep breath.

CHAPTER 22

The next day, David's assistant, Katrina hung up after the 10th phone call from David's mother. The worry she heard in his mother's voice was filling her with the same concern. It wasn't like David to go out of pocket like this. His arraignment was yesterday morning and it was already 2:00 p.m. today. That was more than 24 hours. Yesterday, when he hadn't returned calls, Katrina assumed David had retreated to his Malibu mansion to be surrounded by the people closest to him. But today, the people closest to him were calling Katrina looking for him. They all said they had called him several times yesterday and today, but his phone kept going to voice mail. Katrina had been in contact with the staff at the Hollywood Hills house but none of them had heard from David either. She was nervous. She walked over to the butler, Bernard again.

"What should we do? David's missing."

"He's not missing Katrina, he's just taking time to himself. He had a very stressful day yesterday." Bernard was always the levelheaded one. Whenever there was a problem in the house the staff always went to him and he would take control of things.

"But, it's been so long, Bo." Everybody called him "Bo" for short. "David never does this."

"David's never been charged with a crime either, especially nothing like this. Give the man some time. He'll turn up."

"I don't know Bo, I'm real worried. You know the court made him wear that ankle bracelet to track where he goes. Do you think we should see if they can locate him for us?"

"Are you out of your mind! We are not going to ask the police to track him!"

"Why not?"

"Well, what if he is somewhere he doesn't want to be found! And how would that look, if his own staff were reporting him missing? They'll think he fled!"

"I'm sorry. You're right. It was a really dumb idea. I'm just so worried about him. This is why I always come to you first."

"Has Pierre made David anything to eat?"

"But David's not here."

"He will be. Just you wait and see. I know he'll be coming here to ride out this storm. I want to make sure everything is prepared for him and he receives a very warm welcome from us all when he comes home."

Katrina went into the kitchen looking for the chef. He had already prepared a feast. It was 2:00 p.m., but Chef Pierre had everything available, from breakfast foods, to lunch and even steaks. There was David's favorite style cinnamon and sugar french toast with fresh berries and crème fraiche. There were eggs benedict, chicken and waffles, smoked salmon, Caesar salad, roast beef, filet mignon, french fries, roasted potatoes, and ceviche. It looked like a brunch fit for a king. Katrina smiled. Of course nobody would have to tell Pierre to get cooking. He was already prepared to give David a warm welcome and a full tummy. And he was nervous too. He was just as worried as Katrina was. And when Chef Pierre was worried, he cooked.

"Ka-trina!" Chef Pierre said with his thick French accent. "Has David come home?"

"Not yet. Chef Pierre."

"Did he call!"

"No."

"Then I must bring out the warmers. I must keep the food warm for when he arrives. I bet you he has not eaten a thing in 24 hours!"

"That's a good idea. He'll appreciate that."

Katrina then went upstairs and tried to busy herself to keep from worrying. It didn't work. She found herself calling all of David's friends to see if they had heard from him. Then finally, she heard the loud roar of a Lamborghini's engine. She knew it was him, but she looked out her window anyway to be sure.

"It's David!" Katrina shrieked as she went running down the stairs. "He's here, everybody! David is here!" She was like an overly excited child at Christmas time. She was so relieved he was ok. All the staff were. They all came rushing into the living room and had gathered in a semi-circle around the front door by the time David opened the door.

"Heeey. What's going on?" he asked, with a smile on his face.

Katrina threw her arms around him. "We were worried about you! Everyone is!"

David returned Katrina's hug. "Why? I'm fine. What's all the fuss about?"

"You didn't answer anyone's calls. You're mother's worried sick. We were all worried."

"Not me," said Bernard. "I knew you just needed time to yourself but I couldn't get these people to calm down."

David looked around at everyone, happy to see how much they cared. It was nice to receive this warm welcome home.

"Let's eat!" declared Chef Pierre.

David's face lit up. "Yes. Food. I'm starving. I hope you all will come join me."

Everyone did. When they all walked in the kitchen, David exclaimed: "What!? What's all this for?"

"You," said Chef Pierre. "I knew you probably did not eat. I did not know what you are craving right now, so I prepared all your favorite foods."

David's heart warmed at the kind gesture and he smiled. "Thank you. This is fantastic. Katrina, call my family. They should come join us. But we don't need to wait. We can get started. They'll just have to catch up with us, when they get here."

While he waited for his mother and his siblings to arrive, David enjoyed a wonderful meal with all his staff surrounding him. They laughed, they teased each other, they discussed current events, and they all enjoyed Chef Pierre's amazing food. David declared that he was giving them all the rest of the day off and insisted that they drink champagne with him. And they all did. David looked around at the jolly crowd and thought to himself. "*This* is my family." And they were. David's staff cared about him. They worried about him. They nurtured him. And they had each been there for him for several years. He watched their kids growing up. They all made him Christmas cards and called him "Uncle David."

Bernard had been with David from the beginning. He was David's first butler in New York. He moved to L.A. with David when David left New York. He was properly placed in David's central hub in Beverly Hills, because he was the one who kept the wheels greased on everything. He made sure all the administrative matters of the household were tended to. He was essentially the supervisor of all the other staff, both in this house and in Hollywood. He was also the point person when David would need him to send over a cleaning crew and grounds keepers in Malibu. Bernard knew nobody invaded David's sanctuary unless David gave the word they were needed there, and Bernard served as the gate-keeper, sending staff when David wanted them, or keeping them away to protect David's private sanctuary. Bernard was the eyes and ears of all the households. And he kept a close eye out for things that were not in David's best interest, and he would immediately solve the problem. He had even advised David of past girlfriends' activities that he knew David wouldn't approve of so that David could make the right choice about the girlfriend in question.

Katrina was not only David's personal assistant taking all his business calls, arranging his business meetings and handling his correspondence. She was also the one who called the doctor when he was sick, and made him go. She was the one who scheduled all his dentist appointments and made sure he kept them. She was the one who would stock his bathroom mirror with vitamin C so he'd remember to take it during flu season. She paid attention to his health and she kept him healthy. And she was his friend. She was a good friend. She was more than a personal assistant. She was also a personal friend. All his staff were. Katrina was a single mother, so David would sometimes accompany her to her child's play or little league game. He actually enjoyed it. And he liked it that her kids called him "Uncle David."

Chef Pierre was the one who prided himself in keeping David well fed. He was a jolly man, rotund in shape, with rosy-red cheeks. And he loved food. He couldn't stand to watch anyone be deprived of good food. It was his philosophy that food was one of life's greatest pleasures, and to be denied that pleasure was like being denied life itself. David chuck-led now as he watched Chef Pierre adding more food to David's plate. David remembered a time when he tried to hire a nutritionist and per-sonal trainer to get him in shape, but Chef Pierre refused to abide by her dietary restrictions. David was walking past the kitchen one day when he heard shouting.

"No!" Chef Pierre had shouted. "I will not deprive David!"

The personal trainer tried to stand her ground, "He is paying me to get him healthy and in shape."

"I am the one who keeps him healthy!" screamed the Chef, "You! You, want to make him like a twig! *That* is not healthy!"

"Should he be fat, like you!" the personal trainer fired back.

David had stopped in the doorway of the kitchen but hid himself from view. He would not take sides. He wanted to see who would win the argument on their own. Part of him hoped that Chef would win, but he was afraid that would mean harder workouts from the trainer. So, he decided he would just endure the result of whatever compromise the heated conversation would yield. He was amused listening in. It was more heated than many of his business negotiations over multi-million dollar deals. But ultimately, the Chef and the trainer had reached a compromise they could both begrudgingly live with. And David did lose weight on that diet, and without having to suffer too much either. Of course, Chef Pierre knew which days the trainer would not be at the house, and he would sneak in meals outside the compromise on those days.

David looked around at all his staff as they enjoyed a champagne brunch fit for a king, and David thought to himself again, "Yes. *This* is my family." David decided in that moment that he would never again give his heart to another woman in hopes of marrying and having children. He never wanted to have his heart ripped out of his chest like that again. Instead, he would enjoy this family.

Before they finished their brunch, David's mother and siblings came over. They hugged him and kissed him and scolded him for not answering his phone for so many hours. Then they joined the fabulous brunch and they all enjoyed the rest of the afternoon together.

CHAPTER 23

David didn't leave his Beverly Hills home very often anymore. The media was already reporting on his indictment. So David was laying low for a while. It was too embarrassing to be seen in public now. He knew he shouldn't incarcerate himself in his own home, pending trial, just in case he was never coming out of jail after that, but he just couldn't get himself to go out. He didn't want people to stare and whisper. He didn't want people to ask questions. So it was much easier to just stay home. It was times like this, when he felt cooped up, that he most regretted not being able to retreat to his old sanctuary, with its expansive grounds and lush gardens. He so ached to be in a beautiful place like that, enjoying the outdoors, hearing the birds singing, feeling nature's beauty surrounding him. He longed for that place so badly now, but it also made him sick to think of it. He couldn't think of that place without the image of Sarah entering into his mind. Usually he pictured her happy, smiling up at him in his Garden of Eden; but all that did was make him yearn for what they had shared, and he didn't want to feel that way anymore.

So for now, his rooftop pool at his Beverly Hills home would have to do. David was lying in the sun on a lounge chair when Frank announced his arrival: "Hey Buddy! Pour me one of those!"

The two of them were scheduled to have poolside mojitos this afternoon; and David could really use the time with his old friend Frank.

As Frank and David drank their mojitos, they began pondering David's circumstance.

"I just don't get it David, this doesn't make any sense. How could something like this happen?"

"I don't know, Frank."

"You don't have any enemies. Who would tell a story like this about you? And why so many alleged victims?"

"I don't know Frank."

"You didn't recognize any of the names in the charges the judge read?"

"Not a single one."

"Nothing rang a bell?"

"Well, there was one that vaguely sounded familiar."

"Who?"

"It was a female name, I can't remember it now. I remember thinking it was the only one that even had the remotest sound of familiarity. I think her name was 'Kelly.'"

"Kelly? Kelly what?"

"I can't remember. It'll come to me."

"Ok, so possibly this case has been initiated by a crazy female whose name you can't remember. I guess that's likely."

"I'm not like that Frank! You know I never just toss women to the curb. I always keep a friendship with them, even if I no longer date them. Even crazy Janet. Even after all she's done. I kept letting her come to my parties. I still answered her calls."

"And I told you, you should quit that one -- cold turkey."

"Yeah, I know you've told me. But that's my point. I'm not the love 'em and leave 'em type. I love 'em, then love 'em some more. I don't have a trail of scorned women in my past."

"But you kind of left everybody after you met Sarah. You just disappeared out of the Hollywood scene. And it's been months. Is there anyone you left behind who could be out to get you?"

"I just can't think of anyone. I didn't have a steady relationship for at least two years before I met Sarah. Actually, Janet was the last steady relationship I was in. Everyone else was just a good time; and I never led anyone on to the possibility of anything more."

"Was Janet's name on the list?"

"No."

"Is it possible that Janet got to Sarah?"

"What do you mean?"

"Well, you know how Janet has her way of finding out who you're dating then saying who knows what to make the girl disappear, then show up later angry as hell because of whatever crazy story Janet told her."

"What are you suggesting, Frank? That Sarah has spear-headed false charges against me because of something Janet told her?"

Frank didn't answer, he just shrugged his shoulders and turned his palms up as if to say, "maybe?"

David narrowed his eyes at Frank. He didn't like hearing that suggestion. The two men sat in uncomfortable silence as they continued drinking. David stared out ahead at the water and began pondering Frank's various theories.

He thought of his old life before Sarah, and he tried to imagine who the 'Kelly' girl might be. Then he thought of crazy Janet and how much havoc that woman could wreak. Crazy Janet was stunning. She was a model who had been on the cover of various men's magazines, particularly the ones that featured nude models. She had long thin legs that seemed to reach her neck. She had a tiny flat stomach and extra large false breasts. They were disproportionately large for her extra thin frame, which only made the display that much more exhilarating for a man. Her sleek black hair was always cut short in a bob, with the bottom a sharp edge, always cut perfectly to trace her thin, feminine jaw line. Her white skin contrasted against her black hair, making her pretty little face strikingly beautiful. She always wore bright red, glossy lipstick and jet black eye liner, which made her sharp blue eyes pop in contrast to all the colors - the dark hair, the white skin, the red lips. She was a striking beauty that oozed sex appeal. Actually, just sex. One look at her and all a man could think about was sex. That is how she devoured them. She always reminded David of a black widow, like that. But in the past, he had been a moth to her flame.

He remembered the first time Janet had run-off a potential girl that David had on his arm. It was at one of his parties. David and Janet had already been broken up for 6 months at the time. She was invited to his party as always because David was not aware of any hard feelings. He thought they'd had a clean break. David was having his usual good time, working the room, like the life of the party that he was, until he set his sights on a blonde bombshell that captured his attention above all other women at the party. He courted her and she played coy. He flirted with her and she played hard to get. He charmed her and she warmed up to him. And after a few hours of making her feel like she was the only woman in the world, David invited her upstairs with him. David had a full staff of security guards and servers who would mind the party and shepherd people out when it was time to shut it down, so David frequently took the liberty to retire to his bedroom with one or two beautiful women while his parties kept going on downstairs.

On this day, after a lot of hard work winning her over, David and the blonde bombshell were walking arm in arm up the stairs exchanging sensuous kisses until they reached the top. As David opened the door to his bedroom to let her in, he heard a shout from below by Frank.

"Hey, David, before you disappear for the night, there's someone I want to introduce you to!"

David told the blonde to make herself comfortable and he'd be right back. David hurried down the stairs, quickly greeted the men, and even more quickly excused himself.

"Gentlemen, it's a pleasure meeting you, I'm afraid I'll have to save a more involved conversation for the golf course tomorrow, if you'll join me then, but tonight, I have a more pressing matter that awaits me upstairs."

The men laughed, patted David on the back and said, "By all means, don't let us interrupt." And David rushed back upstairs. He wasn't even gone two minutes, he thought, but when he opened his bedroom door, things had changed drastically from when he had left the blonde there two minutes earlier. The blonde was gone and Crazy Janet was lying naked in his bed. At first David looked around the room, hoping this meant there was going to be a threesome. But there was no sign of the blonde. He looked toward the doorway of the master bath wondering if she was in there freshening up, and as if reading his mind, Janet said:

"She left."

"Why?" David asked. He was frustrated. He worked so hard to get her to his room. She was the only one at the party he wanted. And he wanted her bad. And now she was gone!

"I don't know," Janet said, as she began caressing herself. "But I'm here."

David watched Janet. He was still hard from the prospect of the blonde and he was angry with Janet for interfering. But the things Janet was doing to herself in his bed captivated him. He watched her, trying to decide what to do. He knew he shouldn't reward her for what she had done. He knew he should put his foot down and tell her she had no right to sabotage his chances with another girl. But instead, he stood in his doorway and watched her. He could hear the sound of the party behind him. He could turn and leave. He should turn and leave. Frank had warned him about this vixen. He had told him to sever all ties because she was bad news. But that was easy for Frank to say. She had probably never lied down in Frank's bed and done the things she was doing to herself now.

Janet was stretched out in David's bed with the professional pose of a nude model designed to draw a man in. But this was no still shot. She was moving. Oh, was she moving. Her hands caressing her own body, teasing David's eyes with suggestion, her head tilting backwards and to the side; her eyes pleading with him to come to bed with her. David was defenseless. He shut the door behind him and walked over to his bed.

A week after Crazy Janet had driven off the blonde and lured David into bedding her instead, David ran into the blonde in a coffee shop. She gave him a mouthful. "How dare you!" she screamed at him. "How dare you try to take me to your room, with you're pregnant girlfriend at the same party!" Then she slapped David. "She told me how you left her as soon as she told you she was pregnant. You pig! How could you do such a thing? And to try to drag me into that mess. How dare you!"

David was flabbergasted, "Pregnant girlfriend? I don't have a..." Then it dawned on him. That was how Crazy Janet got rid of her that night. She made up a story to drive the girl away.

David had a series of similar events occur after that, all of which were engineered by Crazy Janet. She was trying to drive all the women away from David in attempt to create a situation where she could force him to be only with her. But when she and David were together she would never try to pressure him into relationship. She would just use her skills of seduction to lure him in. Her work to force him into a relationship was behind the scenes. She would repeatedly drive off other women, then put herself in front of David seductively, and he'd give in every time.

As he remembered these stories, David shook his head at the memory of how masterful she was at that game. Then he began to wonder. Is it possible? Is it possible that Crazy Janet had seen David and Sarah out on the town, completely in love, then approached Sarah with a story so crazy, so atrocious that it pushed Sarah over the edge to seek a vendetta, using her power in the District Attorney's Office to destroy him? Was it possible that his sweet, beautiful Sarah could be that evil? David's heart told him it was not possible; but his mind begged the question: then why did she disappear like that? Why did she abandon me like this?

Then, a name popped into David's mind, "Luthan," he said out loud. "The name I thought sounded vaguely familiar was Kelly Luthan."

"She's a prostitute!" Frank exclaimed.

"What? You know I don't go to prostitutes!"

"Not you, that talent agent. That sleaze bag, Jacob. That's the prostitute he pays to pretend to be his girlfriend. He brings her as his date to your parties!"

David was disgusted. He never had any respect for men who used prostitutes. He never understood how a guy was supposed to enjoy sex, knowing he had to pay the girl to be there. It was always David's philosophy that if a man couldn't charm a woman into his bed, he didn't deserve to have her there. Also, for David, sex was supposed to be a mutual exchange of pleasure. He always pleased the woman first before taking his own pleasure. And if there were two women in his bed, he would please them both before he allowed himself to come. He believed that sex should never be a one-sided exchange where one person took from another -- which is exactly what prostitution sounded like. The whole concept disgusted him. He was even more disgusted that a man could be so pathetic as to pay a woman to pretend to be his girlfriend at a party.

"So how could that possibly have anything to do with me?"

"Think about it David, if Crazy Janet got to her, and she's now out for blood, it makes sense that a prostitute would be among the alleged victims -- someone in the criminal world. Someone Sarah would have easy access to through her work."

"How does that make sense?"

"Well, a prostitute accepts money to do whatever she's told to do to a man."

As Frank's words sank in, they made David feel sick to his stomach. Was Sarah, the woman he once thought would be his future wife, paying a prostitute to destroy him? Could she be that evil?

"I have a headache, Frank. I'm going to go lay down."

"David, you have to make sure your lawyer is aware of all these possibilities, even if it's not true, it could create reasonable doubt."

"I can't, Frank. It's too sickening. Here's his number. Feel free to theorize all you want with him about all the ways to create doubt."

CHAPTER 24

David's lawyer wasn't sure if it was a good thing or a bad thing that his client's girlfriend was standing at counsel table during arraignment. If discovered, it could ruin David's appearance of innocence, especially because she went so light on him.

Also, he did not want to be lured into a false sense of security after the arraignment. For all he knew, the girlfriend was hell-bent on some vendetta she was using the D.A.'s Office to pursue. Hmmmm, maybe he could use that theory at trial if he had to. It could be a surprise attack mid-trial. He would have to work on that strategy. He knew his client was a well-known womanizer. There would have to be a delicate balance struck between showing motive of the prosecuting girlfriend to set up her boyfriend, without giving so much detail that it would make the women of the jury hate him. He decided to conduct polling to see how today's women react to that old saying: "Hell hath no fury, like a woman scorned." He would need to be specific in his polls, identifying the women answering the question by age, race, occupation and other demographics so that he could make quick decisions when picking a jury. He would have to include voir dire questions on the topic as well. Voir Dire was the process that allowed attorneys of each side of the case to ask questions of the potential members of the jury. The purpose was to end up with a collection of 12 of the most un-biased individuals to serve on the jury. However, Dan Goldstein believed that a defense lawyer was not doing his job, unless he was asking questions that would help him identify biases that would help his client and play into the attorney's trial strategy.

David's attorney also considered the possibility that David's girl-friend intended to give him special treatment, or if not, perhaps she could be more easily persuaded of his innocence. There was only one way to find out. Dan called Sarah.

Sarah was deep in thought as she sat at her desk when the phone rang. The sound startled her. She jumped a little as she picked up the phone. It was a voice she recognized well. It was a criminal defense at-torney who was a living legend. He didn't introduce himself before he spoke because he didn't need introduction. He simply asked:

"So, should I tell your boyfriend that you think he's guilty or that you think he's innocent?"

Sarah gasped. She had to catch her breath and regain her composure, and control of the conversation. She knew the abrupt question without introduction was designed to throw her off guard. She decided to buy herself time with a little lie:

"Who is this, please?"

"Come on Sarah, you know exactly who this is *and* who I represent."

"The District Attorney's Office is continuing its investigation. I can assure you that if mitigating evidence is discovered, it will be shared with your office, as required by the constitution."

"Well, what mitigating evidence do you have so far?"

Sarah was not going to allow him to cross-examine her about her own case, while she was unprepared for his call. Still reeling from hearing someone in her professional environment expose the truth out loud, she needed to create distance and time for her to prepare herself for the fact that the defense lawyer knew of her relationship with David. She kicked herself for not having prepared for this. Of course David would have told him about her! She was so stupid for not bracing herself for this moment, she thought.

"Mr. Goldstein, I suggest we meet at your office two weeks from this Thursday to discuss the case. I'm available in the afternoon."

"It's a date! I'll see you here at 1:00 p.m."

As she hung up the phone, Sarah returned to analyzing David's case.

In Sarah's mind, the lack of participation of alleged victims was a sign of David's innocence. People who had been defrauded came forward willingly, and angrily. But these people didn't care? How could that be? Were they even real people? If not, how were the accounts opened in their names? She had to connect those dots. She needed to know who was at the bank each day, opening each of the accounts. She decided to subpoena the surveillance video from each bank for each day the accounts were opened.

The Detective had told Sarah that all the victims had criminal records. So they had to be real people. But she was still determined to watch all the surveillance videos herself--not quite sure what she was looking for. It was Sarah's philosophy that often times in a criminal investigation, you don't know what you're looking for until you find it. So you have to look.

The Detectives had retrieved all the relevant bank statements in the case. Sarah now sat at her desk after a long day in court on other matters, and studied the bank records. She gathered the dates each account was opened at each bank. Since they were all local banks, close in vicinity to the courthouse, Sarah instructed Detective Jones to serve the subpoenas at each bank himself. She asked him to use as much charm and wit as he could to get each bank manager to hand him the video before he left each bank when serving each subpoena.

CHAPTER 25

Sarah was lucky. Detective Jones was able to get all but one video the same day the subpoenas were served. The one that was left would not be available until around noon the day Sarah was scheduled to meet with David's defense attorney.

Sarah watched every single video -- all eight hours of each. The bank records reflected the day each victim's account was opened, but not the time. They reflected cash deposits into accounts opened in the name of each victim listed in the "written confession." To obtain any further information, Sarah had to watch each video, from the time the bank opened to the time it closed for each day a victim's account had been opened. She would spend eight grueling hours watching each video looking for some clue that would point in one direction or the other. She would fast-forward through parts that only showed people lined up in front of the bank tellers. Then she would pause the video, put it in slow motion and zoom in whenever she saw people walking over to the tables where customers would open and close accounts.

Over the next two weeks, Sarah had spent approximately 200 hours, watching all 25 videos. The fact that the victims had criminal histories made things a little easier. She could compare their mug shots to the people who walked over to the area where accounts were opened.

After watching all the videos that were in her possession, so far, Sarah noticed a commonality in each video. In each video, there was a moment where two people approached a table to open an account. In each video, one of the two people would match a mug shot of a listed victim. The second person accompanying the victim, appeared to be the same man in each video. But his face could not be seen.

Though his face could not be seen, the second person had the same build, the same gait, and the same mannerisms, in each video. And he always wore the same baseball cap. It was an over-sized LA Dodgers cap that was pulled down as far as possible, in order to cover his face. In each video, this man held his chin down in an unnatural position the whole time he was in the bank. The unnatural posture appeared to be an intentional act to use the bill of the baseball cap to hide his face from surveillance cameras. Strangely, the man in the baseball cap was always the one handing an envelope to the bank employee when the account was being open. He was the one in control of the cash that was being deposited.

The man appeared to be too thin to be David. Sarah believed that David had a stockier, more masculine build than the man in these videos. Also, the "written confession" stated that the suspect would tell each victim that he was away for weeks. So it couldn't have been David, because it would not fit the M.O. of the "written confession" for the suspect to be at the bank with the victim. It was possible that David was working with an accomplice. The identity of this man could tell the whole story about the entire case. There was something familiar about the man in the video that Sarah could not put her finger on. She zoomed the video as much as possible to view the face, without any luck. She hoped the final video that Detective Jones should be bringing her soon, would show something more.

After Sarah finished watching the last of the videos she had so far, she placed it among the things she would take to her meeting with David's criminal defense attorney, Dan Goldstein. She would take the written confession, all bank records, and one video as an example, and she would describe to Dan the commonality she saw repeated in each video. Of course, he would want to watch them all himself, and the D.A.'s Office would officially provide him all the evidence, but for purposes of this meeting, she would take only what was necessary to review and discuss during the meeting. She was glad she would be meeting Dan in his office. This would take the pressure off and leave her free to explore all possibilities with the defense attorney. In her heart, Sarah wanted desperately to believe that David was innocent. She hoped this brilliant defense attorney would see something she hadn't. She knew that he would try to use her emotions against her to convince her his client was innocent. Therefore, she could trust that he would lay all his cards out on the table. It would not be your typical case, where the defense lawyer saves certain tidbits to surprise the prosecutor with at trial. David's attorney had every incentive to show Sarah everything he had, which tended to convince her that her boyfriend was innocent.

However, as much as Sarah appreciated this opportunity to work with the defense attorney to exonerate David, she also held up her guard. She did not want to be convinced of his innocence, if he was in fact guilty. She could not continue her relationship with him if he was actually a con artist. So while the hope welled up in her heart that David's lawyer would prove to her that David was innocent, Sarah reminded herself to keep her head and not get fooled.

Sarah now gathered her things because it was time to go meet David's attorney. As she was walking out of her office, Detective Jones approached. He had the final video in his hands. She grabbed it from him on her way out and thanked him for his diligent and swift work. She decided she could watch the video with Mr. Goldstein, in his office.

When Sarah entered Dan Goldstein's office, she was escorted to the conference room where he was waiting for her. He greeted her warmly, thanked her for coming and shut the door behind her.

"How are you today, Sarah."

"I'm good, Dan. And yourself?"

"As good as I'll ever be."

"That's good to hear. Shall we get down to business?"

"Absolutely."

"I've brought what the police have termed, a "written confession" which was located in your client's home and obtained through a search warrant..."

"Hold on, hold on, search warrant? My client never told me that a search warrant had been executed. He did mention that his butler told him that two police officers came to visit, but apparently, they did not follow procedure because the butler thought it was just a friendly visit associated with David's enormously generous charitable donations to their causes."

"Let me finish, Dan. I'm not here to argue with you about procedure. If anyone can get evidence thrown out of court, you can. If you have grounds, in due course, I'm sure you will serve your client well. But today, I'm here to go over the substantive evidence with you."

"Fair enough. But I am disturbed by this mention of a search warrant."

"This is the only thing that was seized."

Dan looked at Sarah with surprise. What a strange situation. Police officers usually turned the premises upside down searching for every shred of evidence when they had a search warrant in hand. Now, he's hearing that only one thing was taken, and it was taken in such a way that the butler didn't even notice they were executing a search warrant? In his mind, he was rubbing his hands together at the thought of how much room he had to discredit the investigation, but he decided to save that for a surprise attack. Today, he wanted to get in the prosecution's head. So he let Sarah go on with her version of what the substantive evidence showed. Also, he was relieved to find out that this was the only thing seized. He could really tear this case apart.

Sarah continued, "I also have bank statements that we can review and discuss in a minute, but first I would like us to view a video together. I imagine it will show the same thing I've observed in all the other videos. We have subpoenaed the video surveillance from each bank for each day a victim's account was open. In each video we see a person matching the relevant victim's mugshot walking towards the table to open the account alongside a man who appears in every video, accompanying each victim."

"Let me stop you there for a minute, Sarah. Did you say 'mugshot?'"

Sarah sighed and looked down, as if to concede defeat. Then she picked her head up, looked straight in the defense lawyer's eyes and said: "Yes. Each of the victim's has a criminal record."

"What!?" Dan exclaimed. Then he laughed a taunting laugh. He couldn't hold back. "That's the state's evidence! A list of criminals! Ha! Sarah! What the hell are you thinking, prosecuting this case!"

The defense lawyer's taunting laugh caused the hard-core prosecutor within Sarah to flare up. She looked at the defense attorney, staring straight into his eyes; and with a stern look on her face, and an even more stern tone in her voice, she said:

"Perhaps your client is smart enough to select only victims who will not be believed. Perhaps he is a predator who very carefully selects his prey."

Dan sat up more stiffly in his chair and stared at Sarah. That look on her face, that tone in her voice, he now believed this was a woman out for blood. His client's friend might have an accurate theory. Sarah now sounded like a woman scorned, hell-bent on revenge. He would have to send his investigator out immediately to reach that Janet character. He needed to find out about any contact she may have had with Sarah. But for now, the gloves were off. He was no longer going to handle Sarah like a woman whose emotions might be twisted to favor her boyfriend. He was now going to deal with her as a dirty DA with a vendetta. Dan replied:

"Or perhaps, the District Attorney's Office has threatened these alleged victims and extorted false testimony from them!"

Sarah looked at Dan confused. She was abashed and appalled. What the hell was he suggesting? The thought that Sarah might be viewed as the catalyst of this prosecution had never crossed her mind.

As offended and appalled as she was at his suggestion, Sarah kept her reaction in check. She decided not to inflame the situation any further. So she turned away from him and looked at the large flat screen television in Dan Goldstein's well-appointed conference room, and said: "Let's just watch the video."

Without looking at him, she handed him the video that Detective Jones gave her as she left the D.A.'s Office on her way to meet Dan. It was the last video left to view. Sarah felt Dan angrily snatch the video out of her hands.

As he loaded the video, Sarah said: "You should allow me to fast-forward to the point where I recognize the second person. I will spot him immediately, so we can go right to the relevant portion of the video."

"Fine. You find him, then you give me the remote." Dan snapped at her, distrustfully.

Sarah fast-forwarded with her eyes focused only on the tables where accounts were opened. When she saw the man in the LA Dodgers baseball cap, she slowed down. She then paused to make sure that was the same guy. There he sat, chin unnaturally turned downward, intention-ally hiding his face from the camera.

"That's him," she said. "I recognize the way he forces his chin down so unnaturally as if he is intentionally using the bill of his baseball cap to cover his face from surveillance cameras." She then handed Dan the re-mote.

Dan rewound the video until the point he could see the man and the alleged victim first enter the bank. Then Sarah saw her lucky break. Just as this man opened the door, a gust of wind blew his hat off. "There! There!" she shouted, "Stop the video there! We might see his face!"

The defense lawyer returned the video to that point in time, freezed the frame, then zoomed in. What Sarah saw knocked the wind out of her. First she stared at the video, frozen with disbelief, then the reality of what she was looking at sank in as she heard the defense lawyer speak, his voice filled with the same disbelief she felt. His voice sounding com-pletely perplexed, the words came from his lips with a question of shock: "White Jr.????"

Sarah then fell to her knees and began sobbing. The defense lawyer was even more shocked now. What the hell was going on?

"Sarah? Sarah? What is going on? What does this mean? What con-nection does White Jr. have to my client, or to you! For that matter!"

Sarah was on the ground, her face in her hands as she sobbed, and sobbed. She couldn't form words. In the same moment that she felt relief flood her at the sudden knowledge that her beloved David was innocent, she was also filled with the horror that White Jr., had framed him. She was even more horrified that it was her fault that he was able to do so, because she never reported what White Jr., had done to her. Now, how could she prove White Jr.'s motive? She didn't report the attempted rape when it happened. It wouldn't be believed. David would be viewed as White Jr.'s accomplice and White Jr., would try to negotiate immunity for himself and testify against David. Sarah continued crying, and Dan waited and watched, trying to make sense of the whole scene. He would wait for her to gain her composure before he began asking questions.

He thought the best way to get her composed was to comfort her. So he sat down on the ground next to her and he put his arm around her.

"It's ok, Sarah. I can see this has come as a shock to you. I believe that you are just as surprised to see White Jr., on the video as I am. So take your time. Get it all out. And when you're ready, you will tell me everything. I have all day. Would you like some tea?"

Sarah nodded through sobs and Dan stood to holler at his assistant to bring a cup of tea. He would not leave the conference room out of fear that Sarah might leave. His prime opportunity to get unedited information out of her, was now. This woman had information, and he needed it. Was she having an affair with White Jr.? Was White Jr., setting up his client to get him out of the way? Or were White Jr., and his client somehow connected? Were the two of them engaged in a conspiracy? If so, the only way to get his client out of the line of fire and point the finger solely at White Jr., was to get information out of Sarah, now.

Sarah picked herself up and walked back over to the conference room table. She didn't want the lady bringing her tea to see her on the floor. Sarah dried her eyes and looked down, staring at the table until the tea came.

Sarah held the tea mug with both hands and lowered her face so she could feel the steam, soothing her. She took a sip and Dan Goldstein sat across the table from her. When she put her mug down, Dan asked:

"Sarah, how is my client connected to White Jr.?"

Sarah kept her eyes downward, staring into her mug as she spoke:

"David threw him through a window."

Dan's eyebrows shot up in surprise. He had heard the story circulating around the courthouse that White Jr., was thrown through a window by one of his own clients who tried to rob him, and that White Jr., would not name the client. But he did not believe that David had ever been White Jr.'s client. The answer to his next question was very important. It would reveal whether the incident was a dispute between two criminal conspirators or if some other explanation existed. Dan asked Sarah:

"Why?"

"To save me."

"From what?"

"Rape."

Realization dawned on Dan's face. He was also relieved. His client was not a co-conspirator. Dan was also sorry for Sarah. He now spoke to her with tenderness, "I'm sorry, Sarah. I'm so sorry you had to go through that. I had no idea. Are you ok?"

"Yes. David saved me in the nick of time. I'm ok. But I'm afraid that David will not be ok. I never reported the attempted rape. Now, how will I prove White Jr.'s motive to frame David? The D.A.'s Office will take me off the case. They will treat them as co-conspirators. And you know all White Jr., has to do is offer to testify against David to get immunity. But David has no testimony to give, because the whole story is entirely made up. What are we going to do Dan? What are we going to do?"

"Sarah, is this the original video obtained from the bank?"

"Yes."

"No other copies are in the possession of the police or the D.A.'s Office?"

"No."

"So, right now, you and I are the only two people in the whole world who know what is on this video?"

"Yes."

"We need to keep it that way for a while. We can't let White Jr., know that he's been found out. We need to build our case against him, and in defense of David, before we reveal the contents of this video to anyone. Do you agree with me?"

"Yes."

"Then will you allow me to store this video in my office for safe-keeping?"

"Yes."

"Tell me more about the case. What have the alleged victims said so far."

"Only one has been willing to come forward. The rest have refused to return numerous calls made by the police in attempt to obtain their statements, even with an offer to return a large sum of money that the police have warned them may have been stolen. In addition to the police officers' attempts, I have made calls to all the victims myself. I have left messages telling them we have evidence that a large sum of money has been stolen from them and the only way to get it back is to cooperate with us. But still, nothing. I was beginning to think they weren't real, until I saw them on the videos."

Dan replied: "I assume they will be more willing to speak to a defense investigator than to police or prosecutors, as they all have records of their own."

"I agree."

"My team will get on top of this immediately. We will not allow a single one of these purported victims to avoid our investigators."

"Thank you, Dan. I know you will make this right. Can I ask you for a huge favor?"

"What is it?"

"Can I see David?"

Dan paused.

"I want to tell him I believe he is innocent. I want to explain to him why we can't see each other in public for a while. I want him to know it's not because I don't want to, it's only to protect him."

Dan could see the desperate pleading in Sarah's eyes and it reminded him of the sadness he saw in his own client's eyes. He felt bad keeping them apart, so he said: "I'll need to check with my client to see if he is willing to see you. And if he is, it can only be in my office."

The suggestion that David might no longer want to see Sarah devastated her. That thought had not crossed her mind. Of course, he would've been extremely traumatized by this. It was her he saw as the prosecuting attorney in the courtroom that day, and she had never had an opportunity to explain to him what happened. From his perspective, she just disappeared one day, then the next thing he knew he was charged with a laundry list of crimes carrying up to and over 100 years in prison. How did she not see things from his perspective before? Why hadn't she thought to get a message to him through a trusted friend? She felt so stupid. She felt so cold-hearted. She felt so much regret. She was so afraid that David would not want to see her.

"I'll call him now," Dan said. "I assume I can tell him that you know, without a doubt, that he is innocent and he has been framed. Am I correct?"

"Yes! Yes! Of course!" Sarah said with all her heart.

Dan believed her. He decided it would be ok to leave his client alone in the conference room with her, so they could have a private moment, if he decided he wanted to speak to her.

David picked up on the first ring. His lawyer explained: "David, I have really good news for you. We have discovered the identity of the man who has tried to frame you. But it is not time to celebrate yet. We have a lot of work to do before we reveal the evidence that we have found, which exonerates you. I will explain when you get here. The evidence is strong enough, that you're girlfriend has informed me that, without a doubt, she believes that you are innocent. But she's not the only one I have to convince, because if people discover your relationship, her opinion will not be relied upon and she will have no influence in the outcome of your case. I'm telling you about her opinion because she is here in my office now, and she has asked to see you. David, are you interested in seeing Sarah?"

Sarah held her breath as she waited to hear David's answer. She could only hear the defense attorney's side of the conversation. She heard Dan say, "Ok. Ok. I'll tell her." Then he hung up the phone.

Sarah waited with anticipation and gripping fear.

"He is on his way over here, now."

"Can I stay?"

"Yes. He wants to see you."

Relief filled Sarah's heart, but it was quickly replaced with worry.

"Do you have security guards in the building?"

"Why do you think you need security guards?" Dan asked suspiciously, now angry with himself for having trusted her.

"David tried to kill White Jr., the day he attempted to rape me. I don't know how I stopped him, but I did. When he finds out that White Jr., is also the one who is trying to frame him, he might crack. I want to make sure we can stop him from flying out of here and doing something crazy."

"Pam! Pam!" Dan shouted for his assistant. She quickly came over and Dan instructed her:

"Get two security guards up here immediately. We need them here before the client arrives."

CHAPTER 26

David sped down the highway in his yellow Lamborghini anxious to get to his attorney's office. The attorney had said it was a man who framed him. David clung to that fact for dear life. It meant that Sarah had not set him up. His attorney had said "we" found evidence identifying "the man" who framed you. "We." That sounded like Sarah was assisting his defense! David was so relieved. He couldn't wait to see his beautiful dark-haired beauty again, the woman who stole his heart, the woman he dreamed of marrying and having children with. She was back! His soul mate, the love of his life, was back. She was not the monster Frank thought she might be.

Images of David and Sarah's happy times together filled David's mind. He pictured her giggling in his Garden of Eden. He remembered how beautiful she looked sprawled out naked, lying on that soft blanket where he took her virginity. Her beauty, her purity, so precious in the lush surroundings of the Garden of Eden, she was the woman God created for him. She was David's sweet, darling Sarah. And he couldn't wait to see her. She was waiting for him at his attorney's office, and she knew he was innocent! She may have even been the one who proved it! David's heart was racing as fast as his car was driving. He had to get there, NOW.

When David entered his attorney's office, he greeted him at the front desk, then looked around the room for Sarah. His attorney knew he needed to let the two of them have their reunion before he could have David's attention on the business of the case. So he said, "Sarah is in the conference room down the hall, the first door to your right. I'll let the two of you have some privacy. I'm just a quick holler away when you're ready for me to join you two to discuss the case."

David hurried down the hall. When David saw Sarah, his face lit up with the biggest smile that ever crossed his face. "Sarah, Baby! I love you! Come here!" Sarah rushed into David's arms and the two of them kissed passionately, desperately, as if the air they needed to breathe for survival could only come from their lover's mouth. His arms were wrapped around her. Her arms were wrapped around him. He grasped a thick chunk of her hair and pressed her closer to him. He held her under his devouring mouth. Between kisses, they each gasped as they repeated the same breathy words, "I love you." "I've missed you so much." "I love you." "I never want to be away from you again."

When his desire to kiss the woman he loved was finally satiated, slightly. David held Sarah's face in both hands and he stared into her lovely brown eyes. He needed to see her too, not just kiss her and feel her. He needed to see her beautiful face. So, he held her inches away from him and he just stared lovingly, smiling at her. She smiled back, waiting for more of his kisses.

But the romance of their sweet reunion was suddenly cut short, when David was distracted by what he thought he saw in his peripheral vision. *Was that?* He then looked directly at the image, lifting his eyes away from Sarah's face; he looked over her shoulder at the flat screen TV behind her.

"What! What the fuck! Why is his face on the screen!"

"Oh no! Dan! Dan!" Sarah shouted, "I need your help in here!"

Dan came rushing in with two security guards by his side. As Dan had previously instructed them to do, they each stopped just inside the doorway of the conference room to block anyone from exiting, trapping David, his attorney and Sarah inside. Dan immediately saw what had sent David into a rage.

"Sarah! You left the video up!"

"I'm sorry. I'm sorry."

Dan fumbled with the remote to turn off the screen and remove White Jr.'s image from the extra large frame, as his client continued on, in a rage.

"Is that the piece of shit who framed me! Is that him! I'll kill him! I'll kill that piece of shit!"

Dan tried to calm his client. "David, I need you to calm down. Please calm down. These security guards will restrain you if I decide that is what's in your best interest. I need you to calm down so we can discuss this."

David looked at the security guards who stood together like a solid brick wall closing off the doorway. They each stood with their legs spread apart and their enormous arms crossed, with stern determination reflected in their faces. They were each large enough to be first place heavyweight body builders. Each of their muscular arms were so large they appeared to be larger than both of David's thighs put together, and David was a muscular man himself. There was no way David was getting past that brick wall.

Dan's attorney implored him, "David, please sit down."

David looked at his attorney. He looked at the giant security guards. He looked at the table. Then he looked back at the giant security guards.

Although still too angry to make rational decisions, David was at least rational enough to know he was not getting past those security guards. So he grabbed Sarah's hand and started for the conference room table. The sight of White Jr.'s face was so disturbing. The memory of what he had done to Sarah came flooding into David's mind, so David needed Sarah close. He needed to feel her and know she was safe at his side. David gripped Sarah's hand tightly and pulled her close to him as they walked over to the conference room table together.

Dan sat down across the table from David. He waited a few moments before he spoke. He wanted to see his client visibly relax before he started in about the case. Sarah touched David's arm gently. Her touch always calmed him. As he sat facing his attorney, David let out a long exasperated sigh. That was the cue Dan was waiting for, so he began.

"David, we have good news and we have bad news. The good news is that we have identified the person who framed you. The bad news is it's going to be difficult for us to prove his motive to frame you because Sarah did not report the incident months ago. Bringing it up now, after you've been indicted, raises credibility issues. It could appear as if your girlfriend in the D.A.'s Office is making up a story to protect you. We now have a big job to do. We must locate the alleged victims and get them to testify against White Jr. It is very important that nobody knows we're onto him yet. If he realizes he is on that tape, he will take action to protect himself. We think he will claim it was a conspiracy between the both of you and will offer himself up as a witness against you in exchange for immunity. Before he ever gets the opportunity to push the case in that direction, we need to build a strong case proving that he set you up and you had no idea what was going on."

As David heard his lawyer describe the problems with his case, and as realization set in that the case was far from over, David began mumbling under his breath, "I'll kill that miserable piece of shit, if it's the last thing I do."

Dan knew that his client was in a delicate state of mind. White Jr., had attempted to rape his girlfriend. Then he framed him with the careful strategy of setting up a scenario where the sentences could be stacked to put David away for life. Either one of those things could cause a good man to crack. Any one of those things alone could push a man so far over the edge it could drive him to commit murder. But the two together, that was beyond mention. Dan struggled to find the right words to bring David back to sanity. He needed not only to calm him down for this meeting, but also to make sure he wouldn't allow these things to eat away at him after he left, and trigger him into a violent reaction.

"David, please. Do not do anything rash. Do not disrupt our investigation. White Jr., cannot know that we are onto him. This means you cannot confront him. You have to just wait. Just trust the criminal justice system to take care of him."

David slammed both fists on the table and he stood, shouting: "Trust the criminal justice system!? The criminal justice system is what indicted me for crimes against people I've never met, or even heard of! How does that happen! How can I trust the criminal justice system!"

Dan stood now too. He put his palms up and moved his hands downward in a calming gesture, as if motioning for David to stop, to slow down. Then he spoke: "David, murder is not the answer. You cannot do anything that turns a bad situation into a worse situation."

"How much worse can it get, Dan! I'm facing life in prison! I'd rather spend my life in prison because I wiped that piece of shit off the face of the earth, instead of for no reason at all!"

Tears streamed down Sarah's face. The shame and the guilt she felt were unbearable. It was her fault David was saying these things. It was her fault David was pushed into this vulnerable position and was now fighting like a scared animal for his survival. She was the coward who didn't report White Jr.'s crime. All because of her stupid image that she needed to protect. What a pathetic fool she had been! How could she have let such a criminal escape justice. Now she was being punished for her selfish, cowardly ways by being forced to watch the love of her life suffer like this. She was a prosecutor. She should not have thought of herself. She should have thought only of other victims White Jr., would attack in the future. Though she never could have predicted this, she should have at least thought of other women who might be victimized by a rapist she failed to bring to justice. The tears poured, and poured down Sarah's face as she silently watched the exchange between David and Dan.

Dan realized the stupidity of his earlier words. And he gently spoke, lowering his voice so as to bring down the excitement that was whirling around in the room. He pleaded with his client: "David, I was stupid. I didn't mean to say that you should trust the criminal justice system. But I do want you to trust me. Trust me, David. I'm your lawyer and I'm here to protect you. Trust me to do my job. I have a team of expert witnesses and investigators who have discredited the state and far more reputable victims than the ones the state has in this case. Just trust me. That's all I ask you to do. Stay calm long enough for me to free you of this problem. And trust Sarah. Sarah spent 200 hours reviewing every minute of every video of each business day an alleged account was opened, until finally she found the one frame in all those videos that identified the man who is framing you. We will continue to investigate with the same zeal and determination. We will leave no stone unturned. Together, Sarah and I will build the case that exonerates you and sends White Jr., to prison for a very long time."

At the mention of Sarah's name, David looked down at her. He saw the tears streaming down her face, and it crushed him. His delicate Sarah was crying. Had he scared her? He sat down next to Sarah now and he gently held her face in his hands. He looked into her beautiful brown eyes, which always melted him. And the same way those sweet brown eyes stopped him from killing White Jr., that day, they also released all his tension, all his rage, and all his irrational thought today. He wanted one thing and one thing only, to protect Sarah and make her feel better.

"Sarah, my love. Did I scare you? Don't be scared, Sarah. I didn't mean any of it. I was just angry. But I'm better now. I trust you. I trust you and my defense lawyer to take care of things. I won't do anything Sarah. You know me better than that. If I didn't kill him the day he attacked you, I will never kill anyone. You should understand that. I'm sorry my sweet love. Forgive me for my angry words."

Sarah buried her face into David's chest and threw her arms around him. He engulfed her in the strong embrace of his own arms, as she sobbed with relief into his chest. He held her close and gently rocked her. "It's ok Sarah," he whispered, "It's ok. Everything is going to be ok."

David and Sarah would not be allowed to see each other publicly, for as long as the case was still pending. It would jeopardize the investigation and David's appearance of innocence. The only place it was safe for them to be together was Dan's office. So Dan reserved his conference room for them for one hour each week. Sarah and David would meet there each week and get caught up on each other's lives. They'd giggle. They'd smile. They would hug and they would kiss. But that's as far as the romance would go, as neither one of them had any interest in sneaking a quicky in a law firm's conference room. They each loved and respected each other far more than that. They never discussed the case because this was their precious time to spend enjoying each other, and they did not want to waste or spoil that with the stress of David's case. Sarah trusted Dan to inform his client of everything the client needed to know, so she didn't have to worry about telling David what was happening with his case.

CHAPTER 27

Tom McCalahan had been a criminal defense investigator for 35 years. He worked on the most complicated cases. And when he promised to leave no stone unturned, that promise was kept. No witness was able to avoid him. He always got a hold of them one way or another, and he always got a statement out of them. Often times, all it took was one sentence from one witness that would result in an acquittal. And he knew that well from his many years building the defense case. So Tom always got a statement from everyone on his list of people to investigate, and any name they mentioned, no matter how insignificant it sounded at the time, he would interview. The only time Tom failed to get a statement from a witness was if the witness was dead. If they were alive, Tom McCalahan found them. Today, Dan called upon him. He was the best investigator in the business. Dan instructed Tom to locate and interview every one of the alleged victims listed on the so-called "written confession."

Dan had already had his staff gather all the court files and related data on each alleged victim's criminal history. The information revealed exactly what Dan had already suspected -- each of the alleged victims had been clients of the law firm White, White & Smith. Dan was certain that witness interviews would reveal that White Jr., had either bribed them, manipulated them, or threatened them into going into the bank to open accounts in their names, as he accompanied them holding his own cash that he would transfer into his own off-shore accounts to make it appear as if victims wired money from their own accounts into off-shore accounts bearing the names of false movie titles created by David. He would save the interview of the testifying witness for last. It was obvious that that one was more involved than any of the rest, and was still cooperating with White Jr. But the others had disappeared. They either felt their one task was complete and they wanted nothing more to do with the case, or they were scared.

Now, Tom was out investigating the witnesses. Tom knew how to disguise himself in a way that would allow him to blend in to any witness' environment. If he were going to interview a prostitute, he would pose as a Jon. If he was going to interview a drug dealer, he would watch him for weeks until he knew where and how he transacted business. Then Tom would approach the unsuspecting drug dealer, eager to speak to Tom, hopeful to make a sale. This was trickier because drug dealers were always cautious about under-cover cops, which could be dangerous. So Tom had to be careful not to spook them. He would never pretend like he was about to make a purchase because this would trigger their instincts to watch for something amiss. Instead, he would wait for the drug dealer to make his overture, then he would begin to engage him in conversation.

Today, he was in downtown LA, on a corner where "Ricky" spent a lot of time. Tom was dressed to look like a junky looking for his next fix. He emulated a drug-addict's mannerisms and waited for "Ricky" to approach.

When Ricky approached with his usual: "I got somth'n that can help that twitch."

Tom asked, "What?"

When Ricky described what he had, Tom said, "Nah. I need somth'n better."

"Like what!" Ricky demanded.

"You don't got it."

"If I don't, I'll get it! What's your fix?"

"I'll tell you, but only if you tell me something else."

"What?"

"Are you that guy who ratted out that Hollywood movie-maker for steal'n you're money or somth'n like that?"

"Somth'n like that, what's it to ya?"

"I dunno. Just curious. What'd he do?"

"Noth'n. You want some medicine, or not?"

"What do you mean, noth'n, does that mean you lied about it?"

"Hey! I don't lie! And like I said, what the fuck is it to you!"

"Are you really gonna go to court and testify against someone?"

"Fuck no!"

"Then why'd you tell police?"

"I didn't!"

"Then how'd they get your name?"

"My defense lawyer probably gave it to them. He made me go to the bank so he could deposit some money. I thought he was just hiding his own business, I didn't know he was sett'n anyone up."

"How'd he make you?"

"Fuck you! You ask too many questions."

Ricky then walked away, and Tom knew that was all he was going to get out of him. It wasn't much more than what the video showed. It was obvious from video footage that White Jr., controlled the cash being deposited. Ricky's statement was good because it proved the money never belonged to the alleged victim. But, the taped conversation Tom just had with the drug dealer was not admissible in court. And the likelihood of this guy obeying a subpoena and actually testifying was very low. Although it was good that this alleged victim would not testify (because it would make the state's case harder to prove the crime against that particular victim), the defense team had to assume that White Jr., was going to testify to save his own ass and to continue his vendetta. And White Jr., was sure to testify that the victims gave them their cash in his office, and he merely held it on the way to the bank.

Tom decided to try his luck with the prostitutes. Drug dealers were the hardest people to obtain information from, well not as hard as gang members, so probably, second hardest.

Tom went home, cleaned himself up so that he looked like a decent human being again and then he made his first call. He called the first female listed in the incorrectly named "written confession." Her name was Kelly. He had investigated all the prostitutes on the list long enough to obtain their numbers from somewhere. With Kelly, he had to find one of her old customers and obtain a recommendation from him for a good prostitute. The other women were easier to find than Kelly was. The rest of them had websites where they could be found. But there was no sign of Kelly on the internet. Not on Facebook, not on Twitter, not anywhere. So he had to find her the old fashioned way, through word of mouth, until he finally found his target. Kelly answered her phone:

"Hello."

"Yes. I'm calling to request a house call."

"How did you get my number!" she yelled, angrily into the phone.

"Relax honey, one of your customers recommended you."

"Listen, you pervert, I'm not in that business anymore, so don't you ever call back here again!"

"No wait! That's not really why I called! Don't hang up! I'm investigating a crime."

Out of curiosity, Kelly stayed on the line. She listened.

"Are you still there?"

"Yes."

"First let me say, I'm not the police and I'm not from the D.A.'s Office. I'm working with the defense. I need to ask you a few questions about the case of David Nolan."

"Listen, Mr., I've had a ton of calls from the police, and the D.A.'s Office and now you. I didn't return their calls and I have no intention of speaking to you."

"Why not?"

"Well, I know he's accused of a Ponzi scheme or something. And I know that people who put their own money into those Ponzi schemes can become defendants themselves. So, I'm not going to tell you anything. I'm not even going to tell you whether any of that money was even mine."

"What if all I ask you to do is confirm that it wasn't yours."

"I'm sure there's some type of crime involved in that too, letting someone else use your name to hide their money. No thank you, I'm not getting involved."

"Then why did you get involved in the first place?"

"My defense lawyer paid me very well to take a walk with him to a bank. He said he just needed a beautiful woman on his arm to make him look good. But then when we were there, right in front of the lady, he asked me to sign some papers to put my name on the account. He had a lot of money in that envelope he was carrying, so I didn't care. I thought I would have control of that money. But then right after we opened the account, he wired the money to a different account. By then it was too late. He already used my name. I had no idea what was happening until I saw on the news that David Nolan was accused of stealing a bunch of people's money. Then the cops and the D.A.'s Office started calling me telling me they could get me my money back. Well, I wasn't interested. And I'm still not interested."

"We will subpoena you for trial, then you will have to testify about what happened one way or another."

"Doesn't matter. I'll let them hold me in contempt of court. How much time can they give me for that, six months? It's a lot less than what they could give me for a Ponzi Scheme, or whatever else they would call letting someone use my name in an illegal banking transaction." Kelly was now working as a paralegal, so she knew a few things about the law.

"But if you don't speak, an innocent man's life will be ruined. Think about how you are changing your life. How would you like it if someone tried to destroy you? You're trying to correct your own life. That requires you to do the right thing. All I'm asking you to do, is the right thing. We'll hire the defense lawyer who will represent you to make sure you don't get in trouble for anything you say. Just do the right thing."

"Let me think about it." Kelly then hung up the phone without letting him respond.

The rest of Tom's investigation continued the same way. None of the witnesses were willing to say much and they all swore they would never show up to court. None of them had known that they were being used to set up an innocent man. White Jr., had used bribery and deceit to keep them all in the dark about his true motives. All he had to do was convince them to go for a walk with him. He would let some of them believe that he would allow them to share 10% in the overseas investment he was making, as long as they would let him use their names on the accounts. These greedy criminals were easy targets. They all thought to themselves that somehow, all the money White Jr. was depositing, and possibly more, would end up being all theirs because only their names were being put on the accounts. There was only one exception to this common story -- the testifying witness, who the defense would interview last, after analyzing the other witness' statements.

Tom shared the results of his investigation with Dan. Dan was not pleased. It was not looking good for his client so far. He was still at the mercy of the D.A.'s Office. He didn't have a defense witness who they could count on to show up to trial to exonerate his client. All he could do was piece together the information obtained from the witnesses, hide the fact that they all said they refused to testify, and see if he could convince the prosecution to dismiss the case.

The defense team had reached the point in their investigation where they had to decide how best to use the video of White Jr. Should they interview the testifying witness first and see if they could turn him, or would that tip off White Jr., who would rush to the D.A.'s Office with his own attempts to seek immunity? The more Dan pondered the issues, the more he felt that he needed to present his client first as a witness against White Jr., He had Sarah's testimony about White Jr.'s motive to frame David. His only hope was to trust that the D.A.'s Office would protect their own, instead of a criminal defense attorney. In any other case, he could expect that. But this case was politically complicated. The D.A.'s Office would be worried about its image. They would be worried that they would be accused of allowing Hollywood money, and its girlfriend in the D.A.'s Office, to give a major con artist a free pass. It wouldn't look good for them. Their safer bet would be to prosecute both men who appeared to be co-conspirators, and do what's typical in any case -- give one defendant a lesser sentence for testifying against the other.

Nobody would accuse the D.A.'s Office of favoring a criminal defense attorney; but everyone would accuse the D.A.'s Office of favoring their own prosecutor and her big-money Hollywood boyfriend, who routinely contributed handsomely to law enforcement. The political cards were stacked against David. It was likely that the prosecution would give White Jr., the opportunity for the lesser sentence, instead of David.

CHAPTER 28

A few weeks after her call with Tom McCalahan, Kelly thought about his words. He had asked her to do the right thing. And she knew what the right thing was, but she was scared. She wanted to help David. She remembered him from parties he threw in the Hollywood Hills. One of Kelly's regulars used to take her to all those parties. He would pay her to pretend to be his girlfriend. She didn't think David would ever remember who she was because it was usually just a five-minute conversation where her customer would say: "Have you met my beautiful, girlfriend?"

And David would smile and say: "Nice to meet, you." Only for their short conversation to get interrupted by one of the hundreds of party-goers David was hosting that evening.

The memory of David's face made it harder for Kelly to refuse to assist the defense. David was a real person she could picture in her mind. He wasn't just an abstract thought that could be dismissed easily.

Tom's words haunted her. "You're trying to correct your life, that requires you to do the right thing." But Kelly was only "correcting" her life because she had been caught by the law and that was embarrassing. She wasn't a born-again Christian or anything. She wasn't out to save other sinners or to protect the innocent. She just wanted to avoid getting arrested. She wanted to secret her past from her parents and her family and friends back home, which she could not do if an arrest record followed her. The recent arrest and conviction shocked her back into living a cleaner lifestyle that did not allow for prostitution to pay the bills.

Kelly was raised in a lower-middle class family in Oklahoma. Her parents raised her right and she never had any problems growing up. She never got into trouble, she never did drugs, and she had never been arrested until recently. When she graduated high school, she packed up all her nicest clothes and her piles of makeup. She threw it all into her little, used Toyota and drove to L.A. where she planned on becoming a movie star. Kelly was tall, thin, blonde and beautiful. She had a very pretty face, and she could act. She got all the lead roles in every high school play. This boosted her confidence into believing that she was sure to make it big in Hollywood one day.

But the harsh reality of LA life was brutal. It was expensive there! You couldn't work as a waitress and pay for your own apartment. If you were just waiting tables, you had to have lots of roommates to help pay the bills. And although there was plenty to do, the nightlife was expensive too. One drink could run you $20. It was much harder to live in L.A. than it was to live in Oklahoma. It was even harder to pursue your dreams of becoming an actress while trying to earn a living. Kelly went to hundreds and hundreds of auditions, hoping to land a role. Auditions were often scheduled during Kelly's shifts. So she frequently got fired for too many no-shows at work. This was another reason she had to live with roommates. At times they were all working, at other times, only half of them were working. So the roommates would cover each other while some of them were out of work. It was not the glamorous life Kelly had imagined she'd have when she moved to L.A. So when temptation called for an easier way to make fast money, Kelly gave in.

It happened one day when she was sitting alone at a bar, after an audition. She was still dressed in full hair and makeup and looking like a beauty queen. A bar patron kept staring at her. Kelly thought nothing of it because she got stared at a lot. So she ignored him. Slowly but gradually the man made his way closer to her. He introduced himself and Kelly was polite. He was not attractive and was far too old for Kelly to consider dating, but he was not repulsive-looking either. He was just out of Kelly's typical age-rage. She was barely 21 then and would not consider dating a guy who looked 40. But he was friendly, so she chatted with him. During their conversation, he told her he was a business traveler and that life on the road was lonely. He told her he came to L.A. regularly and was hoping he could see her again. Kelly politely declined, but he persisted.

"I wouldn't expect you to be monogamous with me. You would only be my girlfriend on the days I'm in town."

Kelly snickered. "That doesn't make any sense."

"I can make it make sense for you."

"What do you mean?"

"Well, you're an actress, right?"

"Yes."

"Did you get that role you were trying for today?"

"No."

"How about last time you tried, did you get the role, you wanted?"

"No."

"When was the last time you got a role you wanted?"

"I haven't yet."

"And when did you say you moved to L.A.?"

"Three years ago."

"That's a long time to wait for a role."

"It takes years, though!"

"It doesn't have to sweetheart." The business traveler moved in closer now, putting his hand on Kelly's knee, leaning his face in closer to hers, he whispered in her ear: "I can give you a lead role, right now."

Kelly didn't quite understand what he was saying, so she asked: "Playing, what?"

"My part-time girlfriend, silly. I'll put you up in your own apartment. You don't have to be faithful when I'm not here, just be available for me when I am here."

Kelly looked at him as she considered his proposal. He knew he almost had her, so he smiled at her warmly and caressed her thigh, as he whispered: "Come on, baby, I promise to treat you like my princess whenever I'm in town."

The man's proposal didn't sound like prostitution to Kelly. It sounded like a guy picking up on her for an extended (though part-time) relationship. It just happened to be a relationship that came with perks. Kelly thought about how much easier life could be if someone else covered her apartment expense. She thought of how much more energy she could put into her passion of becoming an actress if she didn't have to hold down a job. This thought made her push the envelope a little further, when he whispered in her ear, "How else can I convince you, sweetheart?"

Kelly asked: "What about spending money?"

The man smiled with the triumph of a conqueror, "Oh don't you worry, I'll give you spending money. Come on, now." He grabbed her hand and Kelly followed him out of the bar.

That was how it all started. The money came easy, so Kelly spent it easily. She was not maintaining a job, so she had to figure out how to get more cash when her business traveler was not in town. That is when she admitted to herself what her arrangement with him really was -- it was prostitution.

Because she had already crossed that line, she didn't see any harm in picking up more business travelers in bars for a little extra cash. She saw no difference between what she was doing and what other women with loose morals did when they had one-night stands for free. But Kelly was careful. She was not a streetwalker. She sought her customers only in expensive hotel bars. She became an expert at recognizing loneliness from across the room. She would find a man sitting alone, staring down at his drink as if he didn't have much to talk about or anyone to talk to. She would target these men and she was usually right -- her target was usually a business traveler who spent too much time on the road to develop a relationship. And these men always had lots of money to spend.

Kelly did not want to get caught, so at first, she focused only on the business traveler. She would always cajole him into showing her his driver's license so she would know for certain he was from out of town and not an under-cover police officer. As the years went on, Kelly also developed a small client base of local men, but only those she already knew, like the man who paid her to pretend to be his girlfriend at David's parties. She will forever regret the day she went out in search of a new business traveler but got sloppy and didn't flirt her way into seeing his driver's license. That was the one and only time she failed to do it. And wouldn't you know it, he was an under-cover police officer. That was how Kelly became White Jr.'s client.

It had been over a year since Kelly had engaged in prostitution. She stopped after she had been arrested. As long as she had been able to keep that part of her life a secret, she was able to maintain a sense of denial in her mind about what she was actually doing. But once she was arrested, she couldn't deny any more the reality of her conduct. During her court appearances, the shame, the guilt and the self-disgust all settled in. She now spent her days trying to forget that she ever supported herself in such a disgusting way.

Now, as Kelly pondered her next steps in life and the conversation she had with Tom, she thought of David's smiling face surrounded by the lively atmosphere of a party. She remembered him as a nice guy. She didn't want to let him get wrongfully convicted. Kelly thought for a long time about what she should do. But ultimately, she decided the only person she needed to take care of was herself.

Kelly was ready to leave LA, giving up on her dream of becoming an actress, but she needed enough money to start a new life back home. It was no longer possible for her to apply for jobs because that would trigger a background check, which would reveal that she was convicted of prostitution. She could never let anyone back home know that about her. The only way she could go back home was if she had enough money to start her own business.

One of her childhood friends had been talking about opening a coffee shop for years. The friend had told her that if they could somehow come up with $100,000 they could do it. Kelly thought of this conversation she had with her old friend, and she knew what she had to do. She was going to pay White Jr., a visit.

CHAPTER 29

White Jr., sat at his desk gathering files when his phone rang. The receptionist announced a call from Kelly Luthan. "Give me a second." He closed his office door for privacy then answered Kelly's call. Her sultry voice instantly made him hard. Kelly was attractive, and she was a prostitute. He hoped she could help him with his fantasy. After his experience attempting to rape Sarah, he developed a taste for the thrill of over-powering a struggling woman who refused him sex. He did not succeed with Sarah, so now he had this reoccurring fantasy of successfully raping a woman.

Sometimes he would visualize himself over-powering a woman in the parking garage who absent-mindedly walked to her car. Sometimes he'd fantasize about Sarah, and what it would've been like if that asshole hadn't come in like that and interrupted his perfect position over her. But White Jr., was also afraid of the consequences. It was only his obsession with Sarah that clouded his judgment and caused him to attempt to rape her. Other than that, he was clear-headed enough to understand the risks involved. And the risks were too high. But now, as he listened to Kelly's sultry voice requesting a meeting with him, he had a great idea. He could just pay a prostitute to pretend to be his rape victim.

"Can I come see you at your office today?"

"No, I was just leaving for lunch. Why don't you meet me at my house in Beverly Hills, instead."

"Ok." Kelly didn't think twice about meeting a man in his home. She had done it many times before.

When Kelly knocked on the door, she was wearing her typical short, almost spandex-like tight dress that barely made it past her rear-end. She wore six-inch high heels. She was dressed all in white from head to toe. Her very long blonde hair fell down her back and below her breasts, and she wore a lot of makeup. She carried a large handbag, which doubtlessly was full of junk. Though Kelly had changed her occupation, she had not changed her style. White Jr., wished she hadn't looked like such a prostitute. This fantasy would be better if she were dressed conservatively and looked more innocent. He decided he could make that request for their next meeting.

"Come on in Kelly, make yourself comfortable. Can I get you a drink?"

"Sure." Kelly decided she needed him relaxed before she made her proposal.

Each of them made small talk for about half an hour before either one of them was ready to tell the other why they were interested in the meeting. It actually hadn't even crossed White Jr.'s mind that Kelly would be there for any reason other than her typical business. So he kept the conversation flowing because he really wanted this to feel like the rape of an innocent woman, instead of a visit from a prostitute.

So White, Jr., treated Kelly as if she were there only for an ordinary social call. He sat next to her on the couch. He filled her glass when it got low and he filled his own glass too. Then Kelly told him why she was there.

"I need more money to cooperate with you on that David Nolan case."

"You've already played your part, sweetheart. I don't need anything else from you."

"Don't you need me to testify?"

"Not for a while. One witness already testified before the grand jury. It's going to be a long while before there is a trial. These things take time."

"But, you also need me to keep my mouth shut in the meantime don't you."

"What are you getting at?"

"Well, isn't it normal for defense lawyers to interview victims in criminal cases?"

"Yes."

"What if I told his defense lawyer, you're paying me to testify against him?"

Her words caused White Jr.'s anger to flare: "You better not, you little whore!"

"How are you going to stop me?"

White Jr., thought about his options. He could threaten her, but he didn't have anything to hold over her head. It had already been a year since she had completed her sentence and her probation from that one prostitution charge. And it wasn't worth it to use violence. She was a whore who could easily be discredited. He would just explain that she was trying to extort money out of him. White Jr., still had no idea that Sarah and Dan had seen his face on the video at the bank. And he believed he'd covered his tracks too well in the financial transactions to worry about that. White Jr., said:

"I'm not going to stop you. You're going to stop yourself. The defense cannot buy your testimony to favor them. But you know, when the time is right, I will pay you to testify the way I need you too. So, what's in it for you? Why would you tell the defense anything that favors them?"

"But I need the money, now."

"How much do you need?"

"I need $100,000."

"Ha! ha! That's a lot of money! Why would I give you that much?"

"Because you'll go to jail if I tell the defense, or the police, that you've created this whole story out of thin air."

"First of all, you're a convicted whore. Nobody will believe you. Second of all, how are you going to explain your way out of the crime you committed while helping me? There is no upside for you in this. So forget about it. I have a much better idea. Why don't you just earn the money you want from me?"

"I'll earn it by keeping your secret."

"That's not what I was talking about."

White Jr., then reached up Kelly's dress and cupped her vagina. "I meant earn it, like you normally earn your money." Kelly shoved his hand away.

"How'd you know that's what I wanted?"

"Shut up you freak! I don't do this anymore!"

White Jr., kept grabbing at Kelly and Kelly kept pushing his hands away. "fff! ooooh! I get so hard when you do that! Yes. keep struggling, I like that."

"Stop it, you sicko! Stop it!"

"If you struggle for me like this every time, I'll pay you a $1,000 each time. You'll have your money in no time."

"I'm not role-playing! I'm telling you, I don't do this anymore! Get your hands off me!"

White Jr., realized she was serious. She must've reformed herself in this past year. That made things even better, he thought. She was his true rape victim. Her fight was honest. If he wanted her, he had to overpower her. He felt the thrill rise up in him. This was perfect, nobody would believe a whore got raped. So White Jr., grabbed her and shoved her beneath him. She struggled to push him off her, kicking him off with both feet. She rolled around and reached for her bag on the end table. He thought she was reaching for her phone. So he grabbed her and pulled her downward away from her bag. He reached one hand around to reach her pussy. Oh, it felt so good to touch what she'd been denying him, he thought.

But his filthy touch brought up all of Kelly's feelings of guilt, shame and disgust from the years she worked as a prostitute, and she turned all her anger over those feelings against White, Jr. She had to reach her bag.

White Jr., worked his finger in her pussy, as she pulled and pulled at his hand to get it off her. His grip was too tight so she began crawling towards her bag again. Her movement in that direction only forced his finger deeper into her, but she had to reach her bag. He was too heavy to get away from, but she could inch forward just a little each time. He was now lifting her dress and pulling at the back of her G-string. He shoved his dick hard into her. The thrust forced her body forward so that she could reach her purse. She grabbed for it and reached the strap, it was now in her hands, as he pulled her backwards with both his hands on her hips, shoving her hard onto his dick. She quickly pulled her knife out of her purse and slashed it across his face. "Oww!!!!" White Jr., jerked backwards instinctively and grabbed his face with both hands. That gave Kelly her chance to run. She ran out of his house as fast as she could, the knife still in her hand. She flung it into her purse as she jumped in her car and sped away.

Kelly had to think fast. She just used a knife against a guy who worked for a highly reputable law firm in town. He was the son of the owner. She had to tell her story first. She had to let the police know she acted in self-defense. Nobody would believe her if the investigation started as an assault case against her. She couldn't be on the defensive. She had to be the first to report the incident. Kelly knew nobody would believe that a convicted prostitute got raped, but she had to convince someone. As she drove towards downtown she remembered that it was a lady prosecutor who had left messages for her about the David Nolan case. Her name was Sarah Cartwright. She would go to her. A woman would be more understanding. The male chauvinistic police officers would never take her seriously. They might even arrest her as soon as she finished telling her story. She had to go directly to Sarah Cartwright.

When Kelly arrived at the D.A.'s Office she demanded to see Sarah Cartwright.

"What is this regarding, ma'am?" asked the receptionist.

"Never mind what it's regarding. It's urgent and it's important and I have to speak to her NOW!"

"I need to know what it's regarding, ma'am."

"It's regarding the David Nolan case and it's regarding another more serious crime by the guy who's framing him! I need to talk to her right NOW!!!!"

Sarah emerged from her office at the sound of the commotion she could hear down the hall. She thought she heard someone say "the David Nolan case" and "the guy who's framing him." She hurried down the hall until she saw a victim she recognized from one of the mug shots. "I'll take it from here, Sandy," Sarah said to the receptionist. She then turned to Kelly.

"I'm Sarah Cartwright. Can I help you?"

"Yes. I need to talk to you it's urgent."

"Come with me."

Kelly and Sarah walked down the hall to Sarah's office and Sarah shut the door.

Kelly pulled the knife out her bag. It still had blood on it. "You're going to need this. It's evidence."

Sarah was more shocked at how Kelly got through security than she was at the fact that the woman had just pulled a bloody knife out of her purse.

"Ok. Calm down for a minute. Place it on the desk here. Now tell me what happened."

"I had to cut Richard White, Jr., the young White from White, White & Smith, because he tried to rape me."

"Just a minute. Let me call a Detective in here."

"No! A man will never believe me. I need to talk to a woman!"

"It's ok. This man takes instruction from me. And I'm a woman. I lead crime teams he serves on. I will make the decisions about this case, not him."

Sarah couldn't be the only witness to this conversation. She needed a detective in there with a tape recorder. Sarah called Detective Jones. He was there in five minutes. Detective Jones introduced himself, bagged the evidence, and started the tape, then he let Sarah take over the interview.

"Ok, miss, now let's resume your report. First, now that we have the tape rolling, we need you to state your name and spell it."

"Kelly Luthan. L-u-t-h-a-n."

"Tell us why you're here today, Kelly."

"Richard White, Jr., tried to rape me. The only way I could get away from him was to stab him with this knife. I swiped it across his face and he let go of me and I ran."

"I hate to ask you this sensitive question, but it is important for legal reasons, so I must ask you. Did his penis penetrate your vagina?"

"Yes."

Sarah needed the answer to that question because it was the difference between rape and attempted rape. Rape carried a longer prison sentence.

"Ok, please go on. Where did the knife come from?"

This question triggered Kelly's quick, street-wise mind. She knew it would make her look guilty if she brought the knife to his house. So she explained: "The knife fell out of my purse during the struggle. I keep it in there but only for self-defense. When he saw it, he said he was going to kill me with it after he finished raping me, so I grabbed it. Lucky, I got to it first. I slashed his face and he let me go, so I ran. I got out of there as fast as I could and I came straight here." Kelly lied. She didn't know what the rules were for using a knife against a man who tried to rape a woman, but she knew that a knife could be used in self-defense if someone was trying to kill you, so she told them White Jr., threatened to kill her. She continued on to make the threat of murder more believable.

"I went to his house to tell him I didn't want to testify anymore in that David Nolan case. He tricked me into opening that account. I didn't know he was using it to frame someone. But when you kept calling, the police kept calling, and the defense investigator called, I put it all together. White used me to frame this guy. So I went to his house to tell him I was going to the police. That's when he attacked me. He said nobody would believe someone who was convicted of prostitution, so he forced himself on me to teach me a lesson, I tried to hit him with my bag to get him off me, and that's when the knife fell out. When he saw it, he said "And I'll kill you after this, so you can't talk either!"

By this point in the interview, Kelly had already said enough to have White Jr., immediately arrested for rape with a deadly weapon and attempted aggravated murder. But Sarah needed all the detail she could to make Kelly's testimony credible, and to exonerate David completely. So the interview went on for another hour. When it was concluded, she gave Kelly information about how to be in touch with the victim's advocate program and she gave her her own business card.

After Kelly left, Sarah looked at Detective Jones and said, "Do not concern yourself with that woman's criminal record. I guaranty you that what she has said is true. I know it not only from the frazzled look and demeanor of a woman who has just experienced trauma, something I trust you observed as well. But I also know it because White Jr., tried to rape me once." Detective Jones' mouth dropped wide open and he stared at Sarah. Then his face turned tender with concern.

"Oh my God, Sarah. Why didn't you say anything?"

"It was a mistake, I know. And I regret that mistake now, but also I now understand why many victims of sexual assault never come forward. I can't explain it now. I was in a different mind-set at the time. The important thing is that we must bring him to justice, immediately."

Sarah also filled Detective Jones in on the video surveillance she observed at the bank, which corroborated the rape victim's story, regarding White Jr.'s framing of David Nolan. Sarah did this in a fifteen-minute briefing, so as not to delay the arrest of White Jr. She told Detective Jones that as soon as he was finished with the arrest of White Jr., the two of them needed to interview the one and only testifying witness in the David Nolan case.

Detective Jones said: "We'll do that immediately. I'll call his parole officer and find out what days he reports."

CHAPTER 30

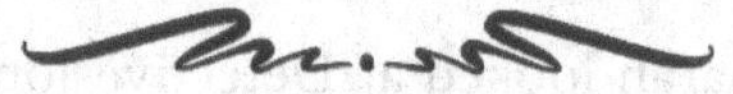

The morning after White, Jr., was arrested for raping and attempting to kill Kelly, Sarah and Detective Jones walked purposefully and with determination towards the office of the parole officer. The testifying witness in David's case was scheduled to report that day. Instead of reporting to his parole officer, he would be answering questions from Sarah and Detective Jones.

Sarah had already given Detective Jones every detail of David's case, including her relationship with David, so that he would be prepared to take a good interview of this final but very important witness. She trusted Detective Jones to keep it a secret for now and to not make any inaccurate judgments about her with regard to her relationship with David. He had a very high level of respect for Sarah, and trusted her completely to handle an investigation properly. He had even said to her: "If it were me in your shoes, Sarah, I would've done the exact same thing."

Now, as they walked towards the room in which they would be interviewing the testifying witness, Detective Jones reminded Sarah: "Ok, we cannot taint the interview with suggestions of what we expect him to say. This has to be a very clean recorded statement that reflects the witness gave us all the information from his own mind, in response to open-ended questions. It's important in every case, but especially this one because of the history you've recently informed me of. You're too close to the case, so you need to let me lead the interview. You're here only as the DA who grants immunity. I'll do the rest."

When the testifying witness walked in, his parole officer said, "We're going to do something a little different today. Instead of you answering my questions, you will be answering their questions."

The parolee saw Detective Jones' uniform and panicked.

"What the fuck!? Why? I haven't done anything."

"Sit down, or I'll revoke your parole for failing to report to your parole officer," said the parole officer.

"Shit," said the witness. He sat down and listened.

Detective Jones read him the Miranda warning and told him the conversation was being recorded. Then he explained:

"You're lawyer has been arrested, and we think you know why. I have a Deputy D.A. with me. She has the authority to grant you immunity, whatever you say. Just tell us how you were involved with the lawyer's scheme."

"Can you give me more details than that, man?"

"No. Either you have answers or you don't. We will not tell you what to say. We will judge the veracity of your statements based on how your statements match the evidence we've already gathered. And we've gathered a lot. Surveillance videos, all kinds of things. To the extent the evidence implicates you, you will be prosecuted to the fullest extent of the law. But if you cooperate, you will be given immunity."

"How much immunity do I get?"

Sarah spoke: "100%"

"No matter what I say?"

"It has to be the truth."

"I mean, no matter what crime I talk about when I tell you the truth."

"Yes. 100% immunity no matter what you confess, so long as you speak truthfully, and testify truthfully, in all proceedings we subpoena you for regarding your statement."

"Is this about how my lawyer, Richard White framed that guy?"

"You tell us." Detective Jones said, as he took over the conversation.

"Well, that's the only thing it can be! I've never had any other lawyer include me in his crime. Can you prosecute him for what he did to me too?"

"What did he do to you?"

"He threatened me! He said if I didn't help him frame this guy, he would make up stories and plant evidence to get my parole revoked! So I had to do what he said! I had no choice! I couldn't believe it, my own lawyer threatening to send me to prison, on false evidence!"

"What did Richard White, Jr., tell you to do?"

"He told me to frame that Hollywood guy. That big movie-maker dude."

"Give us specifics."

"He gave me a thick document. He told me I had to break into his house and leave it on the table. He told me right after I did that, I had to go straight to the police and tell them that he convinced me to invest a lot of money into a movie. He told me I had to tell them that I saw the document when I was visiting him in his home, and that when he went to the bathroom, I flipped through it and saw that he confessed in writing that the movie was fake. That he planned on keeping the money for himself."

"And did you do all those things?"

"Yes."

"And did you testify to all those things before the grand jury?"

"Yes."

"And was that testimony false?"

"Yes."

"Is this the document you planted after breaking into that home?"

"Yes."

"Whose home was it?"

"David Nolan's."

The interview went on until Sarah and Detective Jones were satisfied that they obtained every detail necessary to prove that the witness was describing the framing of David Nolan. They had the witness provide the address of the home he broke into, which matched the address of David's house in the Hollywood Hills. They had him describe how he got around the staff, to which he explained: after watching the house for several weeks, he noticed the staff were never there on Sunday, so that's when he broke in and left the document. They had him read out loud from several pages of the document so that the audio recording would prove he was talking about the same document the police had seized. He complied, and even better than that, he said:

"That's the exact one I left there. It's not even a copy. I know because I was eating a peanut butter sandwich in the car and I got peanut butter on the document. And there's the stain I left. It's still there. This is the exact document that I planted in David Nolan's house."

Today was a very good day. Sarah walked out of that parole officer's office with a light heart and a happy smile. Finally, the burden of David's case was over. She had only two more things left to do.

The timing of the interview of the testifying witness could not have landed on a better day. This afternoon, a status conference was scheduled in David's case. So, Sarah went straight to her office and typed up a Motion to Dismiss the case, with prejudice. She called Dan Goldstein and explained that the testifying witness had confessed on tape to planting the evidence and lying in grand jury, all because White Jr., had threatened him if he didn't obey his specific instructions on how to frame David. She told Dan that she would be dismissing the case at the status conference today. Dan was over-joyed.

"I'll call David!"

"Ok, but I don't want him in the courtroom when this happens. Tell him to go to the Sheriff's office to get that ankle bracelet off and I'll meet him in Malibu."

Sarah wanted a passionate reunion with David in their special place. She also wanted to protect David for a little while longer and not allow their relationship to be revealed in the courthouse the same day she dismissed his case.

When the judge called David's case. Sarah stood and addressed the Court:

"Your honor, I am here today with a Motion to Dismiss and a corresponding order, that we respectfully request you sign at this hearing, right now. An innocent man has been falsely accused. The one and only witness who testified at grand jury has confessed that his testimony was false and that he planted the only physical evidence that exists to implicate the defendant. All other alleged victims either refused to testify, or have directly stated that the money that was allegedly stolen from them, was not even theirs to begin with. It seems that justice requires you to dismiss this case immediately."

The judge did not need to hear from defense counsel: "Bring the order here Ms. Cartwright, I will sign it right now."

Sarah turned her head to find Detective Jones standing in the doorway. She nodded at him, and he understood her command. He quickly exited the courtroom to communicate with the Sheriff's Office that the order was signed and David's ankle bracelet needed to come off, immediately.

Sarah shook Dan's hand and Dan thanked her profusely. "You did a good job, Sarah! You did a fantastic job!"

Sarah thanked him and graciously excused herself. There was something very important she had to do before she could go meet David.

Sarah walked over to the District Attorney's Office but the District Attorney was not at his desk. So she left her resignation on his chair. And she walked out of the District Attorney's Office with the lightness of a woman who had just unloaded years' worth of a heavy burden. She was on her way to see the man of her dreams and she was never looking back.

CHAPTER 31

As Sarah pulled into the drive, she saw David standing outside. She got out of her car and rushed into his arms. They exchanged a long, full body, passionate kiss that made Sarah's knees give way. David held her, strong in his arms, and he leaned her against his Lamborghini. Sarah ran her fingers through his hair and moaned with pleasure. She wanted him to take her right then and there, but she also wanted to thrash around with him in the comfort of his extra-large, soft California King bed.

But then David surprised her.

"Let's go," he said, as he opened his car door.

"Where!?" Sarah asked a little exasperated. All she wanted to do was to finally make love to him, but now they were leaving?

"It's a surprise, Sarah. You're going to like it."

"Ok."

Sarah trusted David implicitly, so she obeyed his instruction to get in the car. She wondered where they were going as they headed towards Santa Monica. Soon she realized what direction they were taking. They were heading towards that small airport in Santa Monica where only private planes fly from. As realization dawned on her, she smiled. This was very exciting, now she really wanted to know where they were going.

As they walked towards a large, stark white plane that glistened in the setting sun, Sarah saw the name "Mustang" in large letters across the plane. As they approached, David said:

"This is my private plane."

"You own it?"

"Yes. It's mine."

"Why is it called 'Mustang'? You like to drive Lamborghinis."

David chuckled. "It's not named after what I like to drive. It's named after what I like to ride. The wild Mustang is my favorite type of horse. My stable has wild Mustangs that I saved from the Bureau of Land Management in Oregon. Sam's father was a wild Mustang rescue."

Sarah stopped and looked at the plane again. She watched the sun beginning to set behind the view of that grand aircraft as she thought how perfect this moment was. She then looked at David and said:

"My hero! You are whisking me off on your big white horse, that we will be riding into the sunset!"

David loved what she had just said! He picked her up and whirled her around, and kissed her. Then he scooped her up in his arms, one arm under her legs, the other arm supporting her back, as he carried her up the steps into his private plane.

Inside the plane was pure luxury -- enormous soft brown leather chairs that reclined to a flat position, a large flat screen TV, tables and a bar completely stocked with fine crystal drink ware and all the amenities for serving up a good drink. The flight attendants' quarters were sectioned off behind a door between the cockpit and the passenger seating area so that David could enjoy his privacy with his passengers. In the flight attendants' area, was a fully stocked mini kitchen and seating for the flight attendants.

More privacy was available for David and Sarah, in a back room behind the passenger-seating area. It was furnished with a double bed and one nightstand. This plane was set up to maximize comfort for long-distance travel.

After taking it all in, Sarah asked:

"Where are we going?"

"The south of France," David said. "The Cannes Film Festival starts in a month or so, so I thought we would head over early."

Sarah squealed with excitement. "Really David! Really! Are we going to the South of France!? I've never been to France!"

"You're going to love it, Sarah. It's like heaven. The Mediterranean Sea along that coastline has the bluest waters you'll ever see. It's the most incredible thing."

"Oh, David, I love you!"

"I love you too, Sarah."

Sarah couldn't wait for takeoff. She and David sat in their seats, buckled in and they held hands. She looked over to David and asked:

"How long will it take before we can move back there?" She motioned for the bedroom.

David said, "Don't worry. We can start right here." And he moved his hand between Sarah's legs and caressed her vagina through her pants. He pressed his middle finger into the material and burrowed it until he felt her lips separate and he found the spot he was looking for. Sarah tried to push his hand away out of fear that someone would see them, but he was too strong.

"Don't worry, they won't come back here until after takeoff."

Sarah was still worried but his touch felt so good, she now just held his hand lovingly as his finger worked its magic. They were still buckled in their seats. It was only one hand that David used to touch Sarah, but the pleasure it delivered was incredible. She leaned her head back in her seat, as his finger burrowed and stroked and pressed. Her body moved with the waves of pleasure his finger sent through her body. Her pleasure climbed with the height of the airplane as it ascended into the sky. She began to sigh loudly; then, David decided it was time for them to retreat into the bedroom -- even though they weren't supposed to get out of their seats yet. David unbuckled his seat belt, then he unbuckled hers and he whispered: "Come on!" Sarah stood up immediately and followed him.

The plane was still climbing so it was hard to balance. They fell towards the door of the bedroom and Sarah leaned against David for support as he fumbled with the door. It flung open and they both tumbled onto the bed. Sarah giggled and David stood up to get the door shut and locked. Once he secured the door, he tumbled backwards into bed with Sarah. Finally, they could roll around together like she'd been craving for so long. David ripped Sarah's clothes off of her and she ripped his clothes off of him. And the two of them devoured each other with kisses, and licks and touch. When they were both naked, David grabbed Sarah tight and pulled her underneath him. He needed her so desperately. He thrust his manhood deep inside her and she shouted with pleasure. He didn't care who might hear. The turbulence of the plane bounced them off of each other. They reached for each other desperate for more. As Sarah and David rolled around in their loving, passionate embrace during that turbulent plane ride, neither one of them could know in that moment, that they were never coming back.

THE END

Not to stay, anyhow. Sarah had fallen in love with the south of France so much that David bought her a chateau at the top of a high hill in a charming little town, still there from the 13th Century, called Eze. It overlooked the yachts moored in the bay of the Mediterranean Sea and it had a view of the coastline and the water for a hundred miles. David was right. It was the bluest water Sarah had ever seen. And the south of France really was, just like heaven. David and Sarah now made this place their permanent home.

Sarah did not want to leave. So David had to fly all their family and friends to Nice so that they could attend David and Sarah's wedding at the top of the hill in the backyard of their charming chateau in Eze.

And they lived happily ever after.

* * *

Stay tuned for the sequel: "*White Jr.'s Trial*"

ABOUT THE AUTHOR

Summer Augustine is a trial lawyer of 20 years, who began her legal career as a Deputy District Attorney; then later became a civil litigator, handling complex business law cases. She is no stranger to the courtroom or the drama that brings people there. She hopes to share her passion for the law, life and love with her readers through a series of novels, *Prosecutors – LA,* which is also being developed for a television series. (the novels can be enjoyed independently and out of order). Summer Augustine has lived on the west coast of the United States her whole life, including Los Angeles. She loves world travel, art, and history. She spends her free time sipping champagne by the pool, unless her nieces and nephews are visiting, then it's tea parties and remote control airplanes.

To follow the author on her various social media accounts, please visit her website:

SummerAugustine.com

Stay up to date on new releases and special offers by joining her fan club:

SummerAugustine.club

OTHER BOOKS BY THIS AUTHOR

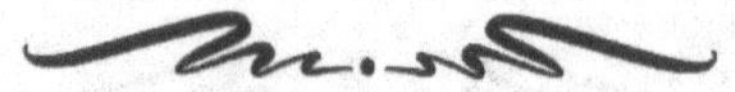

Join the author's fan club for new releases and special offers by visiting: SummerAugustine.club

Available Now:

WHITE JR.'S TRIAL

To find out if White Jr. gets convicted at trial, read: *White Jr.'s Trial* – which *Kirkus Reviews* calls "[a]n engaging courtroom tale" where "high-action danger adds unexpected excitement." Roll up your sleeves and watch how prosecutors and defense lawyers take an entire case to trial. Follow David and Sarah in the South of France, and follow Kelly Luthan in Oklahoma, as Kelly tries to erase her past mistakes to rekindle an old flame, whilst desperately hiding her criminal conviction of prostitution from her fiancé – a secret the subpoena demanding her appearance at White Jr.'s trial threatens to expose.

<u>Coming Soon:</u>

THE SUSPECT

A seductive vixen, whose greatest talent is con-artistry, Venus, is the suspect that Jack Wayne pursues. By the time he finds out, it's too late. Venus has lured Jack into her love web, in a game of winner take all.

THE FRENCH ART HEIST

Their favorite painting is gone! David Nolan stands accused. Who else could have done it? It was Renoir's painting of the future—David's future with Sarah, predicted and painted in 1890. According to David, it depicts the future and the past. Having seen it for the first time in 2015, he swore it captured the most precious moment in David's love story with Sarah when they first met. Livid and out of his mind with rage, the painting's owner demands: "No one else had stronger motive to steal it than David!" There's just one problem – the painting's owner is also David's alibi. So, who really done it?